Beyond the Far Horizon

Ryan,
Happy Valentine's Day!
maybe we can visit some
of the places in this book
this summer.
Papa Ray & Gramma
Nancy

2017

Beyond the Far Horizon

Adventures of a Fur Trader

Charles Cleland

Library of Congress Control Number:		2015919506
ISBN:	Hardcover	978-1-5144-2866-5
	Softcover	978-1-5144-2865-8
	eBook	978-1-5144-2864-1

To order additional copies of this book, contact:
Xlibris
1-888-795-4274
www.Xlibris.com
Orders@Xlibris.com
723222

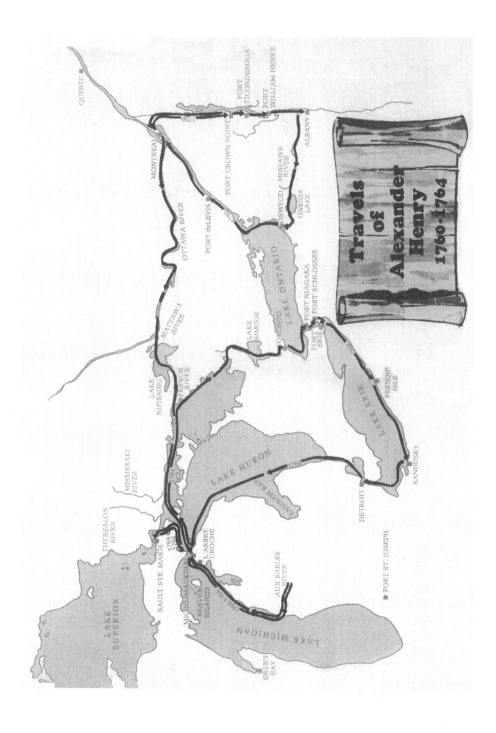

PREFACE

ALEXANDER HENRY WAS a genuine historic figure who
lived a life of adventure as a fur trader during the period
between the beginning of the French-Indian War and the American
Revolution. It is known that Henry was born in the New Jersey colony
in 1739, but little is known of his boyhood. In 1760, at the age of
twenty-one, he left New Jersey to become a trader in the Old Northwest
Territory, which was then Indian country. He remained in the fur trade
for sixteen years, and then in 1776, he retired to Montréal where he died
in 1824 at the age of eighty-five.

In 1809, he wrote and published a memoir with the title *Travels and
Adventures in Canada and the Indian Territories between the Years 1760
and 1776*. Some authors have questioned the veracity of his account
mainly because of a few lapses concerning dates and distances, but
considering that some parts of his narrative were written nearly fifty
years after the fact, when Henry was nearly seventy years of age, his
accuracy and detail are quite remarkable. Apparently, although he
did not keep a formal journal, Henry wrote his memoir from notes
compiled at various times. As a person very familiar with most of the
country through which Henry traveled in the region of lakes Michigan
and Huron, as well as later accounts by other travelers in the same areas,
I believe Henry's descriptions are consistent and accurate.

Henry divided his travel narrative into two parts; Part 1 covers
his activities between the years 1760 and 1765 and mainly takes place
around Sault Sainte Marie, Michilimackinac, and in the Lake Michigan
and Huron basins. Part 2 takes place between 1765 and 1776 and covers
his adventures in the Lake Superior region and on the Canadian prairies
beyond.

After publishing his travels and adventures in 1809, Henry's story
faded into obscurity until 1901 when James Bain published a facsimile
volume. This book was followed in 1921 by an edited version by

historian Milo Quaife, published in the Lakeside Classics series. More recently in 1971, the Mackinac Island State Park Commission issued a version of Henry's Part 1, which was edited by David Armour under the title *Attack at Michilimackinac 1763*.

Although Henry's writing is well-known today by scholars and is frequently cited in the works of both historians and anthropologists, regretfully, it is little known to the public. My objective of producing a fictionalized version of Henry's account is to attempt to make his narrative both more available and more interesting to today's reading public. While I have certainly embellished the story with some adventures that he did not experience, as well as the insertion of dialogue, I have tried to be consistent with Henry's time and character. A section called Historical Notes at the end of this novel will help the reader to separate Henry's fact from my fiction. Hopefully, my own knowledge of the Great Lakes region including its historic places, natural history, and climate, as well as the ethnohistory of its Indian people, permits me to embellish Henry's narrative with scenes and conditions that are, in many ways, as much a part of my world, as they were of Henry's almost two and a half centuries ago.

I am, of course, very much aware of the cultural changes which had already taken place among native people by the time of Henry's visit. The Ojibwe and Odawa people of Henry's day were, of course, influenced by such factors as the introduction of manufactured items, Christianity, and European mercantile economics, yet they also were speaking their native language, living from the land, maintaining traditional social and political practices, and adhering to their supernatural beliefs. Henry's account of his experiences living with the *Wawatum* family for an extended time is one of the earliest, and certainly the most personalized, accounts of some of the cultural practices and beliefs of the Ojibwe and Odawa of the upper Great Lakes area. For this reason alone, it should be more widely known to the general public.

CHARLES CLELAND

ACKNOWLEDGMENTS

G EORGE I. QUIMBY, a distinguished scholar of Great Lakes archaeology and ethnology, certainly knew of Alexander Henry. Over the years, Quimby and I had many discussions of eighteenth-century life on the Great Lakes frontier, and Alexander Henry's account played a major role in our conversations. Quimby, in fact, wrote several articles on Henry's travels with the *Wawatum* family, and his keen insights brought me into a fuller appreciation of the merits of Henry's account. Even though Quimby is now deceased, his influence lives on in my account.

Many others helped in preparing my version of Henry's story, and first among these is my wife, Nancy, who not only made many useful suggestions while I was writing but also spent many hours editing the manuscript. I am grateful for her efforts and support.

Others who read and commented on the manuscript were Ellie Zint, Katie Raymond, Cathy Wigand, Josh Cleland, John Cleland, and Lee Sichter—all experienced writers. I especially would like to thank Betty Henne who brought the practiced eye of a former teacher as well as an invariant reader to bear on my manuscript. All these readers gave help to me in shaping and sharpening Henry's story.

The map of Henry's travels is published courtesy of the Mackinac Island State Park Commission.

LIST OF CHARACTERS

Aamoo (Bee) - Wawatum's boyhood friend

*Akewaugeketauso - Odawa name of Charles de Langlade

*Amherst, Jeffry - commanding general, British Forces

Anangons (Little Star) - Miigwan's wife

*Athanasius - Ojibwe wife of Jean-Baptiste Cadotte

*Belfour, Henry - captain, British Army

*Bodoine, Jean-Baptiste - Saint Lawrence River guide

*Bradstreet, John - general, British Army

*Brant, Molly - Mohawk wife of William Johnson

*Cadotte, Jean-Baptiste - Sault Sainte Marie trader

Campbell, Angus-Sergeant - Highland Regiment

*Campion, Etienne - Alex's fur trade partner

*Cote, Gabriel - Michilimackinac trader

*Desrivieres, Jean-Noel - Michilimackinac trader

*de Langlade, Augustin - father of Charles

*de Langlade, Charles - metis trader and war leader

*de Langlade, Charlotte - wife of Charles de Langlade

Drake, Master - Alex's schoolteacher

*Ducharme, Laurent - Canadian trader, Michilimackinac

*Du Jaunay, Father - parish priest, Michilimackinac

Eddie - army deserter

*Etherington, George - major, British Army

*Gage, Thomas - commander of British Canada

*Goddard, Stanley - Michilimackinac trader

*Grignon, Pierre - Green Bay trader

*Henry, Alexander - fur trader

Henry, Ben - Alexander's uncle

Henry, Collin - Alexander's cousin

Henry, Jock - Alexander's father

*Howard, William - captain, British Army

*Jamet, John - lieutenant, British Army

*Johnson, Sir William - British Indian agent

Jolie - Anagons's mother

Josette - Indian slave, Alex's paramour

*Ledue - French trader

*Leslye, William - lieutenant, British Army

Lonnie - army deserter

*Mahgekewis (first-born) - Ojibwe war leader

Manitou Maaiingun (spirit wolf) - Anangons's father

*Menehweha - Ojibwe speaker

Miigwan - Miskomiigwan's nickname

Miskomiigwan (red feather) - Wawatum's son

*Nisowaquet - Odawa chief

Numge (summer) - Josette's Ponca name

*Ogamachumaki - Odawa chief

Papakin - nickname of Papakinkwe

Papakinkwe (grasshopper woman) - Miigwan and Anangons's daughter

*Pontiac - war chief of Southern Odawa

*Solomon, Ezekiel - Michilimackinac trader

*Tracy, Mister - Michilimackinac trader

Wabigonkwe (flower woman) - Alex's adopted Ojibwe mother

*Wawatum (little goose) - Alex Henry's adopted Ojibwe father

*Wenniway - Ojibwe warrior, nemesis of Alex Henry

Zenibaakwe (ribbon woman) - Anangons's sister

Zhigaag (skunk) - Ojibwe name for Alex Henry

*actual historic figures

CHAPTER 1

ON A SPRING morning in 1760, I, Alexander Henry, the author of this tale, woke from a dream so real, so bizarre, and so alarming that I remember every detail to this day. It is also a dream that I have never related to anyone until now. Likely the dream had something to do with the fact that on that very same morning, I was destined to start an entirely new life. Perhaps the dream had nothing to do with my plans at all, or perhaps it was the portent of my new life.

In my dream, I was at the beginning of a long journey, walking along a path through deep woods. After a time, I noticed that a huge female black bear was preceding me down the trail. At length and for no particular reason, I called out to it, saying, "Mother, wait for me, and we will travel together." As if it was the most natural occurrence, the bear turned, rose on her hind legs, sniffed the air, and looked directly at me. It answered in a language that although totally unfamiliar to me was strangely perfectly understandable. "Yes," said the bear. "Come and join me, and we will walk together."

Without the slightest fear, I hurried forward; and the bear, resuming her four-legged stance, walked at my side. All day we traveled together, chatting casually in our respective languages. As dusk was descending, the bear suggested that we stop for the night. By this time, it was getting dark, so I built a fire. The bear and I had just settled on each side of the fire when an astonishing event occurred. When I looked over at her, I saw that her eyes were glowing bright red; and in that split second, several things happened. I realized that my traveling companion was not a natural bear, and I knew that the bear was deadly dangerous to me. With that, the bear vanished before my eyes; and in that split second, I came fully awake.

I can recall that late spring morning in 1760 very clearly as the day that my life of adventure started. After I awakened from the dream and had a sense of my immediate reality, I can remember being disturbed by the cold breeze that blew through the cracks in the chinking which made up the walls of my bedroom loft. I also remember the soft hooting of a barred owl coming from our distant woodlot. No matter. I shook off the dream and was soon filled with excitement. This was the day I would start a new life, a life which I knew would be filled with adventure and danger.

I peeked through a small hole I'd made in the chinking beside my pallet which served as my own private window on the outside world. The first faint hints of light of the new day cast objects of the farmyard in deep shadows of black and gray. I remember how the things which were the most familiar in my world were cloaked as flat and shadowy forms. It occurred to me then, as it does now, that in the same way, my familiar past on the farm was shrouded by the misty darkness, so my future was also an impenetrable gray. Yet it was this very knowledge which charged my body with excitement.

For all my twenty-one years, my days had been linked to the farm and to coaxing crops of wheat, rye, and hay from the rocky brown soil of the New Jersey colony. Our farm was located near the hamlet of Wyckoff in Saddle River Township, which is thirty miles west of the Hudson River in the northeast part of the colony.

After my mother died of a fever during my ninth year, I was raised by my father, Jock Henry. His younger brother, Ben, owned the next farm. In the life of my father and me, there was only the work of the farm. As a child, I had responsibilities for the care of the chickens, weeding the vegetable garden, keeping the wood box full, drawing water for the household, and doing other chores. From this work, I learned the rhythm of farm life and the unpleasant consequences of failing in my assigned duties. As I reached my teen years, my father began to initiate me into the heavy labor of the farm as we worked side by side, walking behind the plow, hauling stones from the fields, pulling stumps, digging drainage ditches, and stacking hay.

From this labor, I developed a well-muscled body; and by the time I was eighteen, I was nearly six feet tall and weighed one hundred and seventy pounds. My arms and shoulders were particularly strong, and among my peers, there was no one as strong or a better wrestler than me. In addition, my father, who had been a bare-knuckle fighter in his youth, taught me the skills of fighting with my fists; and after a few youthful brawls, there were no other young men who dared to challenge me.

CHARLES CLELAND

Although I was a good worker and took my tasks seriously, and although I did my work well, I was also increasingly bored with the repetitive nature of farm work. As the toil of each season repeated itself year in and year out, I gradually came to dread the thought of spending my life as a farmer. I had no one to talk to about these doubts. My father or Uncle Ben would not have understood my feelings since they were counting on me to follow in their footsteps. This situation grew worse as I gradually began to decide what I really wanted to do with my life.

For whatever reason, I was a person of great curiosity about the world around me and beyond. I'd always paid attention to the habits of wild animals and birds, to landforms and weather patterns, and to all other matters of nature. The more I observed, the more questions arose in my mind about the great interrelated complexities of nature and of human culture. To be sure, this curiosity set me apart from my family and neighbors whose minds all seemed to be focused on the more practical problems of life.

When I was just a young lad, my father enrolled me in the neighborhood school where I became a favorite of Master Drake who taught me to read and write and to become proficient at arithmetic and geography. In fact, it was Master Drake who first interested me in geography and the people who lived in foreign lands. As a young man, Master Drake had shipped aboard a trading bark and had visited many foreign ports. His geography lessons were laced with tales of exotic customs: people who completely tattooed their faces, others who went about with no clothing, and petty kings who had scores of wives and lived in unimaginable luxury. He told of people who ate snakes and bugs and others who feasted on the dogs and yet others who shrunk the heads of their defeated enemies to make trophies the size of large apples. While my classmates squealed with repugnance and disbelief at Master Drake's accounts, I found his stories fascinating, and I began to wonder about the reasons for the strange practices he described. Even though I had never traveled beyond our New Jersey colony, I realized that our own customs, though everyday affairs for us, would seem equally strange and exotic to those raised in a different manner. I longed to actually meet some of these different sorts of people and to learn about their customs firsthand. I was also particularly interested in ciphering and began to dream of becoming a merchant in a faraway exotic land. Such dreams seemed far beyond my reach since my only viable prospects were connected in every way to the farm and the farmer's life.

All this changed suddenly and dramatically when my father was taken by a sickness and died coughing blood during the early winter months. Needless to say, as we were not only family but also working partners and as such, we were very close in every way. My heart was broken at his loss. For several months, I struggled with a deep sadness and the practical problem of how I could work the farm by myself. Then one day, I emerged from my depression, and it occurred to me that I could sell the farm and begin a new life. Fortunately, my uncle was more than willing to buy my land including all our equipment. The money from the sale would provide the funds I needed to set myself up in business as a merchant. Such were my thoughts as I prepared the last breakfast I would have in the only home I had ever known.

As I was taking my first sip of tea, I heard someone hallow the house from the farmyard. Such was the custom, and a wise one where loaded guns were always handy and strangers not always friendly. I, of course, recognized the deep, scratchy voice of my father's younger brother. I unlatched the door and bid Uncle Ben to enter.

"Good morning, Uncle. Would you have tea and some porridge?"

"Aye, Alex and I'd have some talk with you as well if you are of such a mind."

I sat across the rough plank table from Uncle Ben which was at the center of our cabin. The room was dark in the morning cold, but the ever present smell of wood smoke and the crackle and flicker of the hearth fire added both warmth and a bit of cheer.

"Alex, I am very glad to be able to buy this farm from you, but at the same time, I hoped you would stay put and be my neighbor. You know how your father and I always relied on each other when we were in need, and I hoped that when Jock died, you would take his place."

"I'm sorry to disappoint you, Uncle, but I know I am not meant to be a farmer. I mean to travel and earn my living as a trader."

A silence settled on the room as Ben fumbled for his pipe and tobacco pouch and began to pack his pipe with his huge calloused hands. After lighting his pipe with a flaming twig from the fireplace, he studied my eager face as he sucked noisily on his pipe.

"So what is your plan, lad?"

"The last time I visited Wyckoff, the store had posted a broad sheet that said that the British Army was preparing a summer campaign to complete the conquest of Canada from the French. My plan is to leave today and follow the Hudson River road to Albany, and there I will buy goods and a packhorse at that place and then follow the redcoat army that I have heard will be marching to attack Montréal. I hope to sell my wares to the soldiers so I can buy Indian trade goods in Montréal. If the English Army succeeds in conquering Canada, the fur trade of the Upper Lakes country will be open to English traders for the first time. It is my plan to get a trading license and go west to trade with the Indians for beaver pelts."

"That seems like a good ambitious plan, Alex, but in my mind, it has one serious flaw."

"What's that, Uncle?"

"Well, to trade for fur, you have to deal with the red savages, and you will be very lucky to survive when you are in their clutches. I can tell you, Alex, the savages are not human but devils. They are bred to war, killing, and thievery." As Ben talked, his face grimaced, showing the deep emotion of long repressed horrors.

"They are cruel people who live like animals in the forest. They have no mercy."

"But, Uncle Ben, even though I have only seen a few Indians in my entire life, I can't believe that they are totally without humanity," I said.

"You better believe it, Alex. We're farmers. We put the land to good productive use, we don't move from place to place, but we open farms and build towns. We're God-fearing people who believe in love and Christian charity. We are civilized people. The Indians, on the other hand, live by hunting, roaming from place to place. They own no land and neither sow, nor reap. They have no religion, except superstition. They can neither read nor write and have no history. They are not civilized, and that's why we call them savages and barbarians.

"I am not talking from hearsay when I tell you this, Alex. When the Mohawks and the other Iroquois were raiding white settlements in the upper Delaware and Susquehanna Valleys, I was recruited to join the militia to try to protect frontier settlers and their property. In truth, we seldom ever saw Indians, but we did see their work. We would come upon isolated farmsteads which had been completely ravaged. The cabins would be burned to the ground, the livestock killed, and dead and bloated men, women, and children would be scattered about, raped, and mutilated. I will never forget the sights and smells of these wretched little farms. I was seeing the devil's work, pure barbarity." Then he continued in a calmer tone.

"What I find hard to believe, Alex, is that you would leave this beautiful farm and all your friends and neighbors to go into the wilderness and to live by yourself in hardship among cruel and ignorant savages. I'm making an effort to bring you to your senses."

"I'm sorry, Uncle, but I crave a life of adventure and to see new lands and strange people. I want to travel as the spirit moves me."

"Good-bye and fair thee well then, Alex, and God bless you. I will bother you no further but to make you some gifts for your journey."

Then he stepped out of the cabin door and returned with two bundles. I opened the smaller one first and saw it contained a large knife in a beautifully beaded sheath and an Indian war hatchet. The other bundle, long and made of soft deerskin, contained a beautiful Pennsylvania flintlock rifle with a long barrel and a dark walnut stock. I knew that such rifles were made by craftsmen in southeastern Pennsylvania and that in the hands of practiced riflemen were deadly accurate.

"These are from my days in the state militia, Alex. Keep these in hand, and they will serve you well in the days ahead."

I was very touched by my uncle's generous gifts.

"Thank you, Uncle Ben. I will do as you say, and if I have the strength and the wits to survive the wilderness, I will one day come back to visit."

I rode out of our farmyard later that morning on old Millie, my saddle horse, and headed northeast toward the Hudson River. Millie, a beautiful brown-and-white paint, had been my companion since childhood, and although she was now getting old, she had not lost her spirit and was able to sense my every mood. All my worldly belongings, as well as some food for my journey, were stowed in my saddle bags. My bedroll, consisting of two blankets rolled in a piece of oilcloth, was strapped behind the saddle; while my knife, war hatchet, and powder-horn, I wore upon my person. Of course my beautiful long new rifle was in my hands. I should not forget to mention that my money was tucked away in the lining of my boot. Thus turned out, I kicked Millie into a trot, and we were finally off.

Late one day, I came to the ironworks at the new town of Ringwood where a large crowd of miners and wood cutters were at work feeding several smelters to produce badly needed iron for the colonial market. This little town was blanketed by a pale of smoke, and the air held the pungent smell of molten metal.

For the next several weeks, I rode the Hudson River Road to the north. This road, which paralleled the west bank of the Hudson, was little more than a well-used trail that wound its way through a forest of huge old chestnut, hickory, elm, beech, and oak. The interlocking canopy of these giants created a dark green tunnel where shafts of sunlight arrived at the forest floor as a calliope of shifting spots of light in an otherwise dim gallery of trunks. Here and there, forest openings offered views of the Hudson Valley and the orderly rows of green hills which paraded one after another to the distant horizon. The brown river, sliding between its banks below sculpted cliffs, could sometimes be seen, a reminder of the enormous power of the Hudson's waters.

I must admit to myself that despite the majesty of the forest and the beauty of the scenery through which I traveled, the massive green wall of vegetation that surrounded and towered over me induced a claustrophobic fear which was sometimes terrifying. In truth, as a farmer used to long views, to flat open fields and pastures, and to big skies, I knew the forest not at all, not it's shifting shadows, its earthy smells, or the ways of its unseen beasts. Each night I lay in my blankets waiting for sleep while my small fire slowly faded until its diminishing circle of light left me in darkness. It was then that my fears emerged, manifested in the calls of unknown night creatures and their rustling on the forest floor around me. Each night as I waited for the day's exertions to force sleep upon me, I feared the wild beasts, wolves, bears, and panthers; but most of all, I feared the wild and savage red men of the dark forest who now lurked in my imagination—thanks to Uncle Ben's warnings.

Slowly but surely, this forest fear began to fade with the reassurance that came each dawn that found me awake and safe in the same world I left the night before. Just as gradually, my fears were replaced by an enormous curiosity about the new world around me, and my attention was absorbed by learning the songs of each bird and distinguishing the shape and form of each tree and flower. In this way, the unknown was broken down into its finite parts; none of which seemed threatening.

The road north passed through several small settlements whose inns offered some comfort and escape from my open-fire cooking, which, to be honest, was sometimes a disaster. At length, I reached Albany, the largest town in the upper Hudson Valley, which had long been a commercial hub for the Indian trade centered near the Dutch citadel of Fort Orange. That fort, which had been rebuilt and renamed Fort Frederick, was now crowded with thousands of British soldiers preparing for the invasion of Canada.

Although the army's plans were supposed to be secret, after a few days of conversation with some redcoats in a tavern, I learned that two armies were actually being prepared in Albany. One army under Brigadier Haviland, with a force of three thousand four hundred men, was to proceed north up Lake Champlain and then down the Richelieu River to the Saint Lawrence below Montréal. General Jeffrey Amherst, the commanding general of His Majesty's forces in North America, would lead five thousand six hundred regulars, five thousand four hundred Royal Americans, and seven hundred Iroquois warriors, the latter under the direct command of Sir William Johnson, the king's Indian agent to the northern tribes. Amherst's army would ascend the Mohawk River to Fort Stanwix where they would cross the portage to Fort Oswego on Lake Ontario. They would then make their way down Lake Ontario to the Saint Lawrence and then down that river to attack Montréal from the west.

I soon decided that I would follow Amherst's army and become one of the sutlers or independent traders with his huge force. My plan was simple; I would buy goods useful and necessary to the common soldier and sell them on the march and when the army went to winter garrison. Toward this end, I visited several of the Dutch trading establishments that abounded in Albany, and soon I had compiled a sizable array of goods—clasp knives, files, axes, razors, fire tongs, fire steels, spoons, tin cups and plates, mouth harps, lice combs, gun worms, awls needles, and compasses as well as other such items. To carry my stores, I also purchased two packhorses for which I had to pay dearly in this crowded town. At last I was a man of business.

CHAPTER 2

THE TRAIL FROM Albany to Oswego on Lake Ontario leads west and north along the Mohawk River through the country of the five tribes of the Iroquois, the same fearsome Indians Uncle Ben had campaigned against. As we traveled along the river, that is Millie, myself, and the two pack animals, I occasionally overtook marching redcoats and colonial militia also headed for Oswego. Sometimes they marched in good order but were often strung out on the trail for miles. Without fail, the soldiers petitioned me for ardent drink, which indeed I had none, either for my own use or for sale. There were also many troops making their way up the river by whaleboat. Yet despite all the moving men, the trail was a lonely one; and most of the time, I was keeping my own company.

The trail ran along the north bank of the Mohawk River which gently meandered across a broad and beautiful valley. The floodplain along which I traveled was occasionally broken by deep dark ravines containing small streams flowing from the hilly margins of the valley to the river. The valley was entirely forested with giant hardwoods, except for occasional sunlit openings which seemed to have been made by the Iroquois whose practice was to girdle groves of trees to create suitable openings where these avid cultivators of corn, beans, squash, sunflowers, and tobacco could raise their crops. These gardens seemed to be an unkempt jumble of four or five different plants with no order, but as I observed a few of them, my farmer's eye discerned that they did, indeed, have a pattern. Corn and beans were planted in widely spaced mounds so that the bean plants climbed the corn stalks. The runners of pumpkins ran between the corn mounds, in all making a very compact and effective system for growing crops in a small space. This fact didn't seem to square with my uncle's characterization of all Indians as being exclusively hunters.

Once in a great while, I would get a fleeting glimpse of an Indian when they seemed to suddenly materialize along the trail and just as quickly dissolve into the forest as I approached. From the bags and baskets they carried, they also seemed to be travelers along the Mohawk trail.

One evening after I had unpacked and hobbled my horses for the night and was engaged in building a fire to cook my supper, I happened to look up and was shocked to see an Indian man standing not twenty feet from me. I had not seen or heard him approach; it was as though he had appeared from thin air. At first I was so fearful of his intent that I could neither move nor speak. I just sat motionless and stared at him; he, in turn, returned my gaze. This man was about forty years old. He had stern but curious eyes and a rather handsome face. His body was lean and muscular and his bearing entirely confidant. He wore a leather breech clout and moccasins with a red wool blanket draped across his shoulders. His head was bare, except for a strip of short stiff bristles down the middle of his head. Silver bands adorned both his wrists and upper arms; he also wore many silver earbobs. Although he was armed with an old Indian trade musket, which I could identify by its shiny dragon-shaped brass side plate, he did not appear to have bad intentions.

Eventually, I calmed myself and beckoned him to approach, and he responded without hesitation, sitting on the opposite side of my fire. He said something in a guttural language and opened a woven bag he had slung over his shoulder from which he brought out a large dead rabbit. He then proceeded to skin it and place it on a spit over my fire. I put two potatoes in the coals to bake. As we waited for our food to cook, the Indian commenced speaking to me in his strange-sounding language which, since I was in the territory of the five Iroquois tribes, I presumed to be one of the Iroquois tongue; but of course, I did not understand. I told him as much in plain English several times, but it didn't deter him. I, in turn, explained that I was an Englishman and a merchant traveling the Mohawk Trail to Oswego. As I thought about it later, all these facts would have been immediately obvious to him had I said nothing at all. Thus, we chatted on, communicating only that we were both glad for company on our respective journeys.

At length my companion removed the cooked meat and pulled it apart, he then reached into a small skin bag and brought forth a pinch of dried black ants and sprinkled them over the meat. I took the potatoes out of the coals, and we exchanged our respective foods. I was at first reluctant to eat ants but discovered that they imparted a tangy, acidy seasoning to the meat which I judged to be delicious. My Iroquoian guest seemed to be familiar with potatoes, and he ate his with much gusto.

After supper, my guest produced a small clay pipe and tobacco. As he was about to light it from a flaming twig, I produced a fire tong, a device called a smokers companion which was handy on the trail and an item of my trade wares. I used the tongs to pick up a small coal and light his pipe. He was obviously so pleased with this new implement that I gave him the tongs and indicated by hand motions that it was a present. He then removed a silver bracelet from his wrist which bore a beautiful engraving of a lone pine tree and gave it to me. I was equally pleased and smiled broadly as I slipped it on. Although I normally avoid smoking, we passed his pipe back and forth; and I must admit, it seemed to somehow solemnize our companionship.

When my Indian guest finished the pipe, he promptly rolled up in his blanket and was soon sound asleep. I did likewise, and when I awoke at dawn, he was gone. Had it not been for the bracelet on my wrist, I would've thought the whole experience a dream.

A week later, I had progressed upriver past a manor house called Johnson Hall, the home of the British Indian agent, Sir William Johnson, and his Mohawk wife, Molly Brant. Beyond a short distance was the Mohawk town of Canajoharie where the British had recently built a small fortified supply depot. I continued traveling, hoping to soon arrive at Fort Stanwix which guarded the upper Mohawk Valley and the portage to Lake Ontario.

I made camp as usual that night but was in for an unpleasant surprise when I was awakened in the morning by hushed voices. When I opened my eyes, I saw two men examining my goods, and one was holding my long rifle which I always kept at my side while I slept. I jumped from my bedroll and shouted, "What the devil are you doing with my belongings?"

The men turned toward me, and the one with the gun pointed it in my direction. It took me only seconds to conclude that these two were thieves and villains. They were both dressed in what had once been uniforms of the British Army, although they were now filthy and ragged. They were likewise covered with mud and grease, and I could smell them from where I stood. The larger of the two had a deep puckered scar from elbow to wrist, and the other, the one with my rifle, had a pockmarked face and small piggy eyes.

The scarred one said, "Looks like you got more goods than you can use here, boy, and me and Eddie are prepared to relieve you of the lot including this fine firearm."

The other replied, "Yeah, Lonnie, then we can sell him to the Indians for a slave and ride off on these horses."

I was now standing only ten feet away from this pair of no goods, and I knew I had no choice but to fight them. My father's advice suddenly came to mind.

"Son," he said, "if you are confronted by bullies, always choose the leader which, among bullies, is usually the biggest one and hit him as fast and as hard as you can. If you can defeat him, the others will usually run from you."

With this advice in mind, I tensed my muscles and sprang at the one called Lonnie; he clearly was not expecting my move. I threw a punch with the considerable strength of my shoulder which caught him in the solar plexus and drove out his breath. As he bent forward at the waist gasping for air, I grabbed his head and forced it down at the same time bringing up my knee to smash his nose. I heard his nose break as I shoved him backward in a shower of bright red blood. As I turned to see which way Eddie had run, out of the corner of my eye I saw him instead bringing the butt of my rifle down toward my head. I remember feeling horrible pain at the base of my skull and seeing bright lights flash behind my eyes, and then everything went black.

When I awoke, it was almost dark, and the slightest movement of my head brought an unbearable pain. I found that my hands and feet were tied, and I could feel that my shirt was sticky and stiff with my drying blood. I could make out a small fire and could see the two villains sitting beside it drinking from a bottle which they passed back and forth. They looked glum and vicious. I close my eyes and was soon unconscious.

When I awoke again, it was early morning, and I was feeling considerably better. I now found myself in a sitting position tied firmly to a large tree trunk. My head ached, and my vision was somewhat blurry, but I could make out Lonnie with a bandage over his nose and a very swollen split lip. I judged that I was in possession of my faculties since I could now remember with some pleasure my fist sinking into his gut. I could clearly hear the villains discussing their options.

Eddie said, "We have to get on our way, Lonnie. The army is probably on our trail, and we have already been here too long."

Lonnie glanced toward me and replied, "I'm going to kill that damn kid before we do anything else. I'll shoot the son of a bitch where he sits."

"Why don't we just go now and leave him for the wolves and Indians?" said Eddie.

Lonnie replied, "After what he done to me, he ain't gonna live out the morning."

As they sat talking about my fate, I saw a shadowy movement in the brushes behind my captors. With my vision blurred as it was, the movement resolved into an aberration of a huge woman, hair flying, full skirt flapping, as she rapidly closed in on the villains. The figure held a broadsword, and before her prey ever saw her, she brought the flat side of the enormous blade down on Eddie's head and knocked him unconscious. In the next second, she had Lonnie pinned to the ground with the sword point at his throat. She deftly produced cords of raw hide and secured them both, and then she advanced on me; and as she loomed over me, she spoke. After hearing her voice, I was surprised to conclude that the aberration was actually a man wearing a kilt.

"Well, laddie," he said, "you seem to have fallen on hard times at the hands of these cowards and deserters. Let's take a look at your wound." As he untied me, he said, "My name's Angus Campbell, and I'm a sergeant in one of His Majesty's Highland Regiments. My captain sent me to track down these two deserters and to bring them back to Fort Stanwix."

At that point, I spoke my first words since being clubbed. "Thank God you came when you did, Sergeant. They were about to kill me and plunder my goods."

"And who would you be, laddie?" asked the giant Scot.

"I'm Alex Henry, late of the New Jersey colony bound for Oswego to follow General Amherst's army to Montréal as a sutler."

"Just call me Angus, lad. It looks like we are on the same road. I too am bound for Oswego to rejoin my regiment. I'm curious, Alex. Did you give that big lout the broken nose?"

"Yes," I replied, "but I couldn't get to them both."

"Well, I thought that was the case, and do I now see some of the Celt in you, lad?"

I admitted that that was the case, and he smiled broadly.

Later after my goods were collected, repacked, and loaded on the pack animals, the four of us set off for Fort Stanwix. The two deserters led the parade, followed by Sergeant Campbell who encouraged his prisoners from time to time with a knotted rope end. I brought up the rear.

At some point along the trail, I asked Angus how the deserters would be punished once we reached Fort Stanwix, and Angus replied, "Oh, they won't be punished at all. These scurvy bastards will just be shot. We will make an example of them." As much as I despised the two criminals who had attacked me, I must admit that the news that they would be summarily killed sent a tremor through my body.

Two days later, we arrived at Fort Stanwix, a large fortified complex that was partially dug below the ground surface and surrounded by protective earthworks and sharpened pickets. Angus delivered his deserters to the Provost Marshal, and we were billeted for the night. The post surgeon examined my wound, which he cleaned and stitched and then declared that I was fortunate not to have a broken skull. Angus allowed it was because all Scots were hardheaded. The doctor gave me some foul-smelling yellow salve to treat my scalp.

The next morning, Angus and I set off for the portage to Lake Oneida. First, we arrived at Fort Bull, a fortified supply depot at the east end of the carrying place. We then followed the marshy trail along Wood Creek to Lake Oneida where we found soldiers loading equipment into whaleboats for the trip down the lake to the Oswego River. It was here I was obliged to part with Millie and the packhorses. I will admit that parting with Millie brought tears to my eyes and that leaving her to an uncertain fate was one of the hardest things I had ever been required to do. Fortunately, a redcoat major, who was supervising the loading, was more than glad to buy my horses, and the bargain also secured passage for me and my goods to Fort Oswego.

Both Fort Bull and Fort Oswego had only recently been damaged by French and Indian raiders, and the British Army was busy refortifying both posts. As we approached Oswego from the south, the small river opened to a broad estuary. To the east, steep bluffs rose from the river; but on the opposite shore, the hills fell gradually to the floodplain. The plain was covered with innumerable rows of tents that housed

CHARLES CLELAND

General Amherst's growing army of regulars, as well as Loyal American regiments. Beyond, toward the north, were several dozens of small rude houses of the inhabitants of the small village of Oswego. Its few streets were little more than muddy tracks, now deeply rutted by the heavy cannon of the British artillery units. Fort Oswego itself occupied the high ground commanding the shore of Lake Ontario and the mouth of the river. The most amazing sight, however, was on a small peninsula at the harbor's entrance which swarmed with shipwrights who were busy constructing a fleet of whaleboats and barges as well as a larger armed sailing vessel.

Thanks to Angus who was thoroughly acquainted with the procedures of the British Army, I soon received permission to accompany the forthcoming expedition to Montréal and for my goods to be accommodated in three different whaleboats. I was expected to serve as a rower, although I'd never before set foot in a vessel of any kind.

CHAPTER 3

SINCE THE FALLEN hero, Brig. James Wolfe, captured Québec last fall, the city of Montréal remains the only North American city under the control of the French monarchy. Our army, collected here at Oswego, is one prong of an invasion which hopes to take Montréal and with it, all the rest of Canada. In mid-August, we set off down Lake Ontario toward the Saint Lawrence River which we would descend to our objective.

I had never seen so much water as the lake extended unbroken to the northern horizon. It occurred to me that Lake Ontario was more like a sea than a lake. In truth, however, I've never seen the sea; so perhaps for all I know, it would be just as fair to say that the sea looks like Lake Ontario.

On the morning of our departure, I had a fine view of the thousands of departing boats—whaleboats, bateaux, barges, and canoes—all arranged in a huge line extending down the lake until they disappeared from sight. Each vessel was loaded with soldiers, supplies, and the equipment of war. As I watched from a high bluff awaiting the departure of my assigned whaleboat, the countenance of the vista before me transformed from the historic event I'd come to witness to a sinuous black mirage upon the water which could only remind me of a malevolent sea serpent.

Before proceeding further with the story of my voyage, I must say a word about the whaleboat, the craft in which I, in fact, the whole army would spend the next few weeks. As I learned from one of the shipwrights in Oswego, the whaleboat was invented by his Rhode Island ancestors who lived on Narragansett Bay for use from shipboard to pursue whales. They were both small, fast, and, thanks to the double-ended prow, very agile. These vessels were thirty feet in length and about six feet abeam. Rowing was done with very long oars, each pulled by a single man. The whaleboat was not designed to carry cargo, which in our case meant that most of our baggage was accommodated in barges and bateaux.

As a complete landlubber, I had never learned to swim, nor had I ever handled an oar. I was at first very wary of being is such a small boat on such a large lake, but the weather was fair, and the waves came in small swells; and with some hints from the other rowers, I soon fell in with the rhythm of rowing. By the time we reached our first night's camp, my hands, now tender from the lack of hard work over the preceding months, were bloody from broken blisters.

After supper that evening, I decided to look over the camp. As I was strolling among the campfires, I heard someone call my name, and I turned to find myself looking into the smiling face of Angus Campbell.

"Hello, Alex. I see you survived your first day in General Amherst's navy. Come and join me and my messmates at our fire."

I was glad to see my friend and rescuer and to join a half dozen kilted Highlanders. Their thick brogue was difficult for me to understand at times, but they were congenial and full of good humor. Angus and I talked of many subjects that night, and he told me stories of the Highlanders' battle experiences at Ticonderoga and their uneasy relationship with the British Army. I was most interested in trying to understand the relationship between the European armies and their Indian allies, and since Angus was an experienced veteran of warfare on the American continent, I took the opportunity to question him.

"Relations between Indians and Europeans are always complex. Just as the European nations have different interests, so do the various tribes. Perhaps I don't completely understand, but I do know that the Iroquois warriors with us come from the Finger Lake country of the New York colony and that they hate the French. Years ago when the French first came to the Saint Lawrence Valley, they made the mistake of joining a war party of local Algonquian Indians against their traditional Iroquois enemies. This was the first time the Iroquois had seen firearms, and the impact of their use made them permanent enemies of the French."

"So the French Indian allies are not Iroquois?" I asked.

"No, the French allies come from many tribes of the Algonquian people, for example, the Ojibwa, Ottawa, Nipissing, Pottawatomi, Missisaugas, and Abenaki. Mostly these people live in the country of the three upper Great Lakes—to the north and west—the country of the beaver trade."

"Why are they here fighting in the east?" I asked.

"Well, the French give their warrior allies presents and promise them plunder if they join French regulars and provincials against the British. This, the French allies are willing to do, if for no other reason than the British, are allied with their traditional enemies the Iroquois. Also, the French have been their partners in the fur trade which supplies many of the articles and tools that the Indians have become dependent upon for many years."

"So what is the motivation of all the Iroquois to help the British, Angus?" I asked.

"Well, the same thing, presents and the chance to plunder defeated enemies."

"Are these Indian allies good soldiers?"

"Again, Alex, the answer is not easy," said Angus. "In the case of both the Iroquois and the Algonquians, their war leaders have no real authority to order their warriors, so their war chiefs can only make suggestions and to lead by example. As a result, each Indian warrior fights when, where, and how he decides. Obviously, coordination among their fighting men is difficult if not impossible. Apart from that problem, they fight like demons. They are brave, skilled with weapons, raised to withstand extreme hardships, and are crafty fighters; and because they are experts at woodcraft, they are excellent scouts and trackers."

"So the Indians have different fighting tactics from the British and French?"

"Yes," said Angus, "the Europeans like to fight in an open field where closely ranked infantrymen use their Brown Bess muskets which fire a huge .75 caliber ball. When these muskets are fired simultaneously at a range of only seventy-five yards, they create a lead wall which cannot be survived. The Indians, on the other hand, fight from concealment and ambush, situated so if necessary they can fade away into the woods and regroup for another attack. The difference in tactics is why General Amherst does not think he really needs Indians as part of his army." With these new insights to think about, I left Angus and his "black jocks," as he called them, and found my sleeping roll.

Our journey continued on the water so that by the end of the second day, we reached the Saint Lawrence River at the east end of Lake Ontario; on the third day, we began to descend her toward our destination. At its origin, the Saint Lawrence is not a clear and open river but one much crowded with islets of all sizes. These are rocky domes extending above the sparkling green water that swirls silently around them. The islets are covered with luxurious growth of moss and lichen, small shrubs, and very ancient pines which are frequently the aeries of eagles and ospreys that circled squawking overhead as our flotilla passes. Down river from this island paradise, the river runs smooth and unobstructed toward the northeast.

On a small island near the junction of the Saint Lawrence and the Oswegatchie River, the French built and garrisoned a fortification called Fort de Levi. This fort is situated to protect the western approach to Montréal which lies one hundred miles further down the Saint Lawrence. Fort de Levi has a small garrison of only three hundred French regulars and provincial soldiers, but its cannon command the river. General Amherst could have ordered us to portage around the fort and gone on to attack Montréal, but since he is not disposed to have French troops at his rear, he decided to capture Fort de Levi.

As I was traveling near the rear of our column, the attack on the fort had commenced prior to my arrival; this was my first introduction to warfare. I could hear and indeed feel the bombardment of our twenty-four-pound cannon pounding Fort de Levi long before I could actually see it. When I came to the field of battle, I carefully crept to a vantage point to watch the action. Two primal all-pervasive sensations immediately overwhelmed me. The first was a perpetual plume of the acid-sulfur smoke of black gunpowder which hung over the whole scene. This mist of war stung my eyes and invaded my mouth with the taste of hell. The other sensation was a constant skirl of the Highlanders' bagpipes which sent chills up my spine. This was the music, which had long aroused Scottish warriors to valor, but the sound of the pipes also thoroughly terrorized the French defenders who waited inside Fort de Levi's walls for the charge of the fanatical sword-waving Scots.

In fact, many of the buildings inside the fort were on fire, and the once stout log and earth ramparts were rapidly deteriorating under the steady pounding of our heavy guns. As I watched, the over ten thousand men who made up our army began fixing their bayonets to their muskets and preparing to storm the crumbling ramparts; but before this action was ordered, which would surely have been a slaughter, the French commandant wisely surrendered the fort.

When the white surrender flag was raised over the fort the Iroquois warriors, perhaps eight hundred in number, raised the howls of hunting wolves and prepared to plunder the fort and kill its surviving defenders. General Amherst, however, refused to permit barbarous acts and ordered General William Johnson, who led the Iroquois allies, to forbid atrocities. The Iroquois for their part were furious and immediately deserted the battlefield to return to their villages in disgust.

After Fort de Levi was taken, Amherst decided in early September to leave a British garrison behind to repair and man the fort while the rest of his army proceeded downstream to Montreal. The autumn season was now upon us, and the mornings grew quite cold. Maple, aspen, and willows along the riverbanks presented a collage of yellow, orange, and red. If the purpose of our travels could be set aside, the smooth, clear water of the river as it reflected the beauty of the autumn colors would have soothed every evil of the human heart, but, alas, it would have been nothing but an illusion. The Saint Lawrence widened and flowed peacefully until just before the place where the mighty Ottawa River joined it, and here, its demeanor suddenly changed. Now the rushing water squeezes through a narrow channel on the north bank. The river gushes over a series of shale ledges to produce white waters studded with standing waves of great height. This maelstrom is known as the Rapides des Cadres, and it is here that tragedy struck our fleet of whale boats. When I saw and heard the roaring, angry water before me, and especially as I felt a surge of water sucking our boat into the rapids, I was overcome by fear. We rowers, inexperienced with rough waters, quickly lost control of our boat which pirouetted like a crazed dancer until it finally turned sideways in a huge wave which rolled our boat and threw us into the water. As I was engulfed, I thrashed my arms and legs wildly, trying to regain the surface, desperately fighting the water for air and light.

By pure chance, my hand found a mooring rope trailing from our boat, and I managed to keep my head above the water by clinging to it as the boat, now bottom-up, was swept through the foaming rapids. It soon abruptly came to rest on a rocky ledge, and I managed to climb onto the upturned keel. Here, I sat for some hours shivering, as much from fear over my narrow escape, as from the cold. From my perch, I soon noticed the scale of the disaster around me.

Many other boats and their crews suffered the same fate as I and my shipmates. The water around me was filled with overturned boats, struggling men, and bodies of the many who had drowned. At a later time, I learned that the rapids had claimed sixty whale boats and that eighty-four men had been drowned. Much equipment was also lost, including all three boats which contained my goods. Eventually I was rescued by one of the general's aid de camps who had been detailed to assess the damages. It was he who helped me retrieve my long rifle which fortunately I had tied to the ribs of my whale boat. Despite the loss of my goods, I was happy to be alive.

Arriving in Montréal the next day, we found that the city was on the verge of surrender and, with it, all of Canada. At present, however, I had the clothes on my back, my Pennsylvania rifle, some money in my boot, and credit in Albany. I resolved to follow my original plan, that is, to obtain more sutler goods from Albany, which I would then return to sell in the army camps-in order to obtain the funds I needed to enter the fur trade. Eventually I had to acquire Indian trade goods as well as to find out more about the trade itself.

Thanks again to my friend Sergeant Angus Campbell, I made arrangements to accompany an army resupply column, which would ascend the Richelieu River to Lake Champlain and go down the Hudson River to Albany. I arrived without incident in Albany in mid-October where I again engaged my banker and the Dutch merchants. I soon refurbished my supplies, adding this time dried peas, beans, corn, and fruits. In late October, I headed up the Mohawk Trail as before but now hoped to sell some of my goods to the soldiers at Fort Stanwix and Fort Oswego.

It was mid-December by the time I returned to Fort de Levi, which in my absence had been rebuilt by the redcoats and rechristened Fort William Augustus. I intended to proceed downriver to Montréal, and I would give the Rapides des Cedres wide berth. Unfortunately, the winter weather was closing in; and I, weary of travel, decided to stay at Fort William Augustus. The garrison was much smaller than that quartered in Montréal, but on the other hand, this post was more isolated, and its men were short of food and equipment of every kind. I judged that they would be eager customers, and I was not mistaken.

CHAPTER 4

B Y MID-FEBRUARY OF the year 1761, after having spent nearly a year at Fort William Augustus, I had all but disposed of my goods, and I was becoming tired of the monotony of life at this distant outpost of the British Empire. It was, I thought, even worse than the farm; and as a consequence, I decided to go immediately to Montréal. This season's ice floes in the river made water travel precarious, so I engaged a guide to accompany me overland. Jean-Baptiste Bodoine was recommended to me as a Canadian who was well familiar with the Saint Lawrence Valley and conversant with the local Indian dialect, and he agreed to be my guide. At this time of year, the ground was covered with three feet of snow which obliged us to use snowshoes, a device, with which I was unaccustomed but I was told would permit us to walk over the top of the snow.

The snowshoe is an Indian invention. It is shaped like a long oval with a tail, and this form is created by steaming and bending thin strips of wood into the appropriate shape. The interior is then well laced with strong strips of rawhide. The snowshoe is strapped to the foot in such a way that the heel is free to rise and fall with each step while the toe remains tightly fixed. Except where the snow is packed or where it is crusted with ice, the snowshoe normally sinks four to six inches into the snow under the weight of the walker. Were it not for the snowshoe, the walker would sink several feet into the snow and find every step impossibly strenuous. In the years to come, I would spend many days traveling on snowshoes, but my first few days were a disaster. Because of their size, they require a wider-than-normal stride, and the stride must also be somewhat longer. This being the case, as one walks, the forward step can easily come down on the edge of the trailing snowshoe which is often hidden under the snow. In such cases, a fall will surely follow. It should also be mentioned that once I fell with snowshoes strapped to my feet, it was very difficult to rise again. As M. Bodoine and I took the trail north to Montréal, it seemed at first that I fell every dozen steps, but I improved as the day wore on. My leg muscles quickly became sore by the new and unusual way of walking, and I much anticipated the end of the day's travel.

Sundown brought us to a small Indian village of six dome-shaped lodges. The village was populated by twenty warriors and their families, that M. Bodoine informed me, had recently been engaged against the British on behalf of the French. Bodoine spoke their language, and he assured me he knew these men and that I would be safe. Still I was uneasy and insisted that we only stay here for a single night. I was directed to a lodge, where I would spend the night; and being exhausted, I immediately fell into a deep sleep.

While I slept, my traveling companion opened a small keg of rum which he carried in his pack and shared the contents with his Indian friends. I became aware of this after being awakened by a hard kick to my chest. When I open my eyes, I saw my host, a man of perhaps forty years struggling with a young Indian warrior. The younger man had a large knife, and it was apparent that he intended to stab me. As I jumped to my feet, my assailant slashed at me with his knife; and while he missed my vital parts, he did succeed in slicing the palm of my left hand which bled profusely. While my host continued to ward off my attacker, an old woman appeared and, taking my arm, pulled me out of the lodge. I had no coat or snowshoes, nor did I know where to go. The woman let me know by sign that I must hide. For my part, I kept repeating, "Bodoine, Bodoine," and she seemed to understand and that I wanted her to bring him to me.

In the meantime, I hid behind a large tree at the edge of the camp where I watched as several wildly drunk Indians ran from lodge to lodge, presumably searching for me. Bodoine finally appeared, and although he was as drunk as the Indians, he had, nonetheless, thought to procure my coat, gun, and a pair of snowshoes. He secretly took me to the beginning of a hard-packed trail leading into the dark woods and bid me to follow it. Knowing I was in extreme danger, I did so as fast as I could go. After I had walked about three miles, I heard someone approaching behind me and was relieved to find it was Bodoine. I was so happy to see him that I didn't even reproach him for his bad behavior.

We continued walking the entire night, and as light was showing in the eastern sky, we came to a solitary hunting lodge built of sticks which was inhabited by an Indian hunter and his wife. They had a large fire burning and welcomed us into their home. I was quickly reconciled to my second experience with Indian hospitality. We were fed a large meal of venison, and once we were warm and rested, the Indian couple sent us on our way with an ample supply of meat. The gratefulness I felt for the kindness of this small family all but extinguished the experience of our first lodging. So far, my experiences with Indians had been very confusing as their behavior ranged from aggressive and hostile to friendly and very hospitable. I am at a loss to explain these events or their causes. Whether these different circumstances were triggered by my behavior or my nationality or by the political views or ethnic affiliation of the Indian hosts, I do not know. I have no notion as to how future interactions will transpire. I can only be wary.

Bodoine and I continued northward along the south bank of the Saint Lawrence for several days, quite content thanks to the venison supplied by the Indian hunter. But a critical problem arose; we needed to cross the river to get to Montréal and the French settlements. As luck would have it, Bodoine found a birch bark canoe of about sixteen feet in length which had become lodged among a thick stand of willow shrubs along the riverbank. Perhaps it had been abandoned the previous fall by Indian travelers, or perhaps it had slipped its moorings and drifted downstream. On close inspection, we discovered that our craft was in deplorable condition, and we worked all day patching holes and cracks as best we could. Given my previous experience on the river, I was apprehensive to say the least and very reluctant to set foot in this canoe, but there was no other option. To make matters worse, getting our canoe and ourselves onto open water was a challenge. Although the mainstream was free of ice, fast ice clung to the shore, making an apron of ice which was too strong to push the canoe through but not strong enough for us to walk on.

After considerable crashing and cracking and gushing of icy water, we finally got our frail boat and ourselves onto the river. With our makeshift paddles, we got to deeper water, which in summer sunshine was a clear, sparkling blue and so inviting but was now impenetrably black. Our canoe was spouting water from a variety of locations, and we furiously paddled toward the nearest shore. I felt very relieved to make landfall until Bodoine informed me that we were on an island and that we must once again face the black river. More time was spent

CHARLES CLELAND

patching our canoe with small pieces of bark and pine pitch for our forthcoming try to reach the north shore. On this attempt, we did reach our destination despite six inches of icy water in the bottom of our canoe. As the Canadians say, we "encamped" in the spot we landed and tried and tried to warm and dry ourselves with a large fire. This was not made any easier as a blizzard with howling winds descended upon us. We build a driftwood shelter where we huddled together for warmth that night. The morning arrived with a clear sky and a dazzling sun shining on new fluffy snow. The shadows of tree branches on the white snow laced the surface with gray images of what appeared overhead as black limbs against the deep blue heavens.

The country was so desolate that we were surprised later in the morning to see a horse-drawn sleigh moving in our direction. We hailed the driver, and he agreed to deliver us to the village of Les Cedres, which in those days was the uppermost Canadian settlement in the Saint Lawrence valley. Arriving at the village of Les Cedres, I was introduced to the seignior, M. Leduc, who received me with great hospitality.

I learned from Bodoine, who served as our interpreter, that M. Leduc as a young man had been engaged in the fur trade at Michilimackinac located at the junction of Lac de Huron and Lac de Illinois, which in more recent times the latter became known as *Michigami* from the Ojibwe words meaning "large lake." I was very excited to hear about his time in the Upper Lakes country. In the course of our conversation, I learned a great deal about life in what he called the *pays d'en haut* or the country of interior Canada, including its native people and the workings of the fur trade. M. Leduc who, in addition to his native French, also spoke Ojibwe, assured me that the natives of the Michilimackinac region, that is, the Ojibwe and the Odawa, were peaceful and that the fur trade in that country was very profitable. He also told me that the Indians much preferred goods made in England to French-made merchandise because they were both more durable and cheaper. Once I had confessed my strong desire to follow the fur trade at Michilimackinac, M. Leduc highly recommended Etienne Campion of Montréal, a veteran fur trader, as my guide and partner.

After making my way to Montréal, I sought out M. Campion at his home; and after meeting him, I immediately saw the wisdom of M. Leduc's recommendation. M. Campion told me he had first visited Michilimackinac as *a coureurs de bois* or an independent trader eight years ago and had returned on several occasions. On the strength of his personal experience, he was well acquainted with Michilimackinac. He explained that the name Michilimackinac actually applied to the entire region around the Straits of Mackinac. At a time before the turn of the previous century, the French had built a fort trading house and mission on the north shore of the Straits, which is now called Saint Ignace, but that place was abandoned in 1705 in favor of Detroit. In 1715, however, a military and trading post was built on the south shore called Fort Michilimackinac. While it has only a small garrison, each summer, the fort attracts hundreds of traders from all over the country around lakes *Michigami*, Huron, and Superior. They gathered around the fort to sell their furs and to resupply their trade goods for the next season.

M. Campion also assured me that he was well acquainted with many traders that frequent Michilimackinac as well as the Ojibwe and Odawa, the Indians who live in its environs. He said he also spoke some of their language but confessed to being less than fluent. M. Campion also explained that his own ambition was to establish himself as a trader at the south end of Lake *Michigami* near Fort Saint Joseph in the near future.

After our talk, I asked Campion if he would consider acting as my guide and partner for my initial trip to Michilimackinac during the next summer as well as to be my agent in Montréal thereafter. He readily agreed, and I was well pleased by our arrangement. We decided to meet the following summer at Le Chien to begin our journey. With this understanding and the month of May at hand, I again traveled to Albany to procure my fur trade goods.

The goods I purchased for the fur trade differed a great deal from those I handled in my business as a sutler. Working from suggestions of M. Campion, I bought from the Dutch wholesalers many woven fabrics, including wool blankets, shroud, bolts of printed cotton, ribbons, fathoms of glass beads for both necklaces and costume decorations, iron axes, files, knives, hatchets, fire steels, spearheads, arrow points, fishhooks, ice spuds, German silver trinkets, nested brass kettles, lead for musket balls, bullet molds, black Dover gun flints, casks of gunpowder, carrots of tobacco, Italian vermillion, and a few trade muskets. Despite much advice to the contrary, I bought no intoxicating liquors for the trade but did procure a supply of rum for my own use. I also used the opportunity to outfit myself with new clothes, camping gear, and a medicine chest.

CHARLES CLELAND

Fortunately, my earnings selling goods to soldiers had about covered my losses incurred when my boats overturned in the Saint Lawrence. I had now also spent the balance of my account from selling the farm, so I would now be dependent on my success as a fur trader.

I started back to Montréal by way of Lake Champlain and the Richelieu River and arrived without incidents in mid-June. My next task was to secure a trading license from General Gage, who was now commander in chief of all British Canada. As there had been no treaty of peace between the British and the Indian allies of the French, the general did not believe he could guarantee the protection of the property and the lives of His Majesty's citizens on the distant frontier. As I discovered, however, he had already granted one trading license for the Upper Lakes country, and I was compelled to remind him that he could not, therefore, in all fairness refuse me. Thus, despite his better judgment, I received my license to trade at Michilimackinac and its environs on the third of August of 1761. Without further delay, I dispatched canoes to the warehouses at Le Chien at the mouth of the Ottawa River. It was here I was to lade my merchandise and to meet Etienne Campion to begin our journey west.

CHAPTER 5

THERE ARE SEVERAL routes that could be taken to reach Michilimackinac by water from Montréal, but the shortest one and the one used traditionally by the traders who were headed to the Canadian interior was called the Ottawa River route. This route went from Montréal on the Saint Lawrence, north and west up the Ottawa River to its junction with the Mattawa River and hence up to Lake Nipissing. Once across this lake, the route lay over the height of land to the French River which flows west to Lake Huron. From here, the route follows the North Channel between the Canadian mainland and Manitoulin Island and finally south along the shore of the large peninsula which separates Lake Superior from *Michigami* to the place where the waters of Lake Huron and *Michigami* meet at the Straits of Mackinac. Although the Ottawa River route was the shortest, it was also the most difficult owing to the many falls and rapids that had to be portaged. By the time I ascended the Ottawa in the late summer of 1761, the route had been in use by French fur traders for a century or more. Its landmarks were well-known and its traditions well developed. In fact, a whole occupation had grown up around the transporting of freight up the Ottawa River to the *pays d'en haut*. The men of this special profession were mostly French-Canadians voyagers or *engagees* who contracted to take trade goods and supplies to Michilimackinac and other distant trading posts each spring and then to return to Montréal with furs in the autumn.

The device which made this journey possible was another ingenuous invention of native people, the birch bark canoe. During my time in the Upper Lakes country, there were no roads other than a few rude trails. All travel was done by water—rivers were literally the roads in the country—and water travel was exclusively by canoe. The outer skin of the canoe was made from quarter-inch-thick sheets of birch bark, which in making the canoe were placed in a form so that the interior could be lined with ribs, and these were covered with closely spaced cedar wood splints. Like the bark, the interior structure was attached to a wood frame which formed the gunwales; bow and stern posts were affixed to the frame by fine spruce root chords, which the Indians called *watab*. Seams in the skin were sealed with pine pitch mixed with ground charcoal. The genius of the bark canoe was that they were fast, agile, and light and could be mended with readily available materials. My canoes were of a type called *canot due nord* or North canoes, each measuring thirty feet long and four and a half feet wide. These vessels weighed just three hundred pounds so they could be portaged by two men.

As was the custom, my goods were packaged in *pieces* or packages that weighed between ninety and one hundred pounds each. My entire stock was contained in one hundred and eighty *pieces* with sixty *pieces* consigned to each canoe. In addition to the cargo, each canoe carried six paddlers and two-end men who were responsible for steering the canoe with large paddles. The canoes also contained one thousand pounds of provisions, which consisted mainly of dried peas and beans and salt pork and forty pounds of personal baggage for each man. Thus, fully loaded, a North canoe carried about eight thousand pounds or four tons. Three or four canoes, in our case three, under the leadership of a guide, made up a brigade. Our guide was, of course, Etienne Campion who, by tradition and contract, was responsible for any loss of cargo. In addition to M. Campion and myself, there were twenty-four voyagers in our brigade. The voyagers were highly skilled at paddling and portaging, the latter being very important for us. Because of our late start in the season, the water in the river was low, making more portages necessary. In portaging, each voyager was responsible to carry two pieces at a time. For carrying, a trump or burden line, which was, in effect, a headband, was used to help support the first piece, the second being stacked up on the first at the nape of the neck. With this two-hundred-pound weight, the voyagers scaled steep and slippery, rocky portage trails or slogged through the deep mud of marshes. On smooth water, the voyagers could paddle at four miles per hour even against the current. This work was fueled by dried peas and beans and salt pork carried in each canoe. Although this diet was from time to time supplemented by fish and game, the voyagers were too busy to live from the land.

On the lakes, breaks were called once each hour so the men could smoke their pipes while the canoes drifted. Distances were often measured by the number of pipes smoked between specific points; thus, for example, three pipes might be twelve miles. The voyagers were, in general, short, tough, and very muscular men given to cheerfulness and song. When rum or high wine was available, they were also prone to heavy drinking and carousing. Many voyagers had families on both ends of the Montréal to Michilimackinac route: French wives and children in the Saint Lawrence settlements and Indian wives and mixed blood children at Mackinac Island or Saint Ignace at the Straits of Mackinac.

Having said something of the canoes and the stout men who paddled them, I now turn to our eight-hundred-mile harrowing trip to the *pays d'en haut* as the French called the interior of Canada. Montréal is on an island in the Saint Lawrence which is at the head of seagoing navigation because of the Lachine Rapids which block deep water navigation farther up river. The village of Lachine is nine miles upstream from Montreal at the mouth of the Ottawa River and serves as the starting point for canoe brigades headed west. After loading canoes at Lachine and departing, the first stop was the Church of Saint Ann only a few miles away. By tradition, brigades pause here so the voyageurs could attend mass, leave offerings, and get the blessings of the priest for their long and dangerous journey. Once the church service and the blessings were finished, another less dignified tradition took place. Each canoe was provided with eight gallons of rum—one gallon per each man— meant to last for the entire trip. Delayed gratification was not, however, in the spirit of the voyageur; many of our men tried to drink their entire ration the first night.

The following morning, a collection of stumbling, moaning canoe men reloaded our canoes and set off down the Lake of Two Mountains, which is but the estuary of the Ottawa. It is not my purpose to give a full description of our travails in ascending the Ottawa but to at least describe a few of the challenges sufficient to represent the toil and scenery encountered on this route west.

The first night, we camped at the end of the Lake of Two Mountains. On the trip down the lake, we saw no more cultivated land after about twenty-five miles from the mouth of the Ottawa. Above our camp the next morning, we faced the Long Sault, a twelve-mile series of rapids in three sets, each requiring a portage. The portage trail was along the north bank of the river, and we found it both rocky and slippery.

CHARLES CLELAND

Arriving above the Long Sioux, we caught the first site of the granite hills and cliffs of the Canadian Shield to the north, which would be our constant companion up the Ottawa. We also passed two fortified trading houses, one of which was unoccupied, so we helped ourselves to fresh vegetables from its weedy and unattended gardens.

About sixty miles upstream of the Long Sault is the beautiful and dangerous Chaudière Falls. These twenty-five- to thirty-foot falls are given their name because the spraying mist rising from them reminds the voyagers of a boiling cauldron. The mist produces a beautiful, never fading rainbow in the sunshine. The portage was so close to the falls that we got wet from the spray as we passed.

It was at these falls, however beautiful, that I narrowly escaped a fatal accident. A few miles upstream, we were overtaken by a fierce thunderstorm, so we hurriedly pulled the canoes ashore so that we could seek shelter in the dense cedar forests that border the river. Finding a large piece of bark used for patching the canoes, I chose to remain in the canoe covered with my bark roof. Because of the exertion of travel and the gentle splashing of rain on my covering, I soon dozed off. After some time had passed, I awoke suddenly with the sense that the canoe was moving. Looking out, I discovered to my horror that the canoe had escaped the shore and was drifting in the current toward the cauldron. Fighting off a wave of panic, I quickly jumped out of the canoe and found myself in four feet of very fast water; I grabbed the still loaded canoe and tried to hold it against the current. Even with the strength which comes from mortal fear, I could barely hold it. Fortunately, my cries for help brought several men splashing to my aid; and with a great concerted effort, we succeeded in bringing the canoe back to the shore. In so doing, they saved not only my property but also my life for which to this day I feel a great indebtedness.

Further above these falls are three sets of wild rapids, the Little Chaudière and the Deschenes rapids, the latter named for the huge old oak trees lining the shore of these particular rapids. After these portages, our next obstacle was Chats Falls or as the French knew them, Sault des Chats Sauvage, which I am told comes from the many raccoons that frequent this area of the river. Chats Falls is actually a series of about fifteen beautiful falls surrounded by magnificent white pines. The Chats Rapids above the falls extended for five miles, and these were portaged over a large island in the channel.

Above Chat Sault, the river flows around several islands to produce the Chenaux, a series of four rapids. We passed these rapids by a channel on the north side of the river using ten-foot-long poles or *perche,* which are carried for this purpose. They are used by several voyagers who stand in the canoe and use the poles to push against the swift current. Next, we reached the channel of the Grand Calumet which is about twenty miles in length and is named for an outcrop of pipestone at this locale. The Grand Calumet requires four *discharges,* that is to say the freight was offloaded and carried over the portage while the canoes themselves were pulled up by the rapids with long lines. At the head of the Calumet is a one-and-a-third-mile portage which is the longest on the trip to Michilimackinac. This portage is over a hill so steep that twelve men were required to carry each canoe to the summit; the descent was equally steep and dangerous. I was informed that accidents on this portage are common, but fortunately, we accomplished it with only a few minor scrapes and cuts.

At the end of this portage, the greater part of the shallow, rocky portion of the Ottawa is now past, and we paused today to repair canoes. Each canoe carries pitch, bark and *watab* cordage sufficient for necessary repairs.

Above the Calumet portage, we had to portage another series of rapids to reach flat water called Lake Caulonge. Having done so, we passed Fort Caulonge, a fur post on the north bank of the lake. Even further upstream, we came to a sandy point extending into the river. This is called Point Bapteme because it was customary to pull out the canoes here to "baptize" novices of the Ottawa River passage. As the only novice in our brigade, I endured several dunkings and was required to "stand a *regal*" that is to provide rum and other luxuries for the entire brigade.

Above the point was a set of four very turbulent, roaring rapids called Des Joachims which we portaged by two carries, each a half mile in length. After this, we finally arrived at the mouth of the Mattawa River which enters the Ottawa from the west. Our route lay up the Mattawa, which is about forty miles long but has numerous falls and rapids as it flows through the hilly country with much bare rock and stunted pines. Passing the rapids, we were able to paddle across a series of small lakes each separated from the last by a short muddy portage much infested with black flies. This very small creature bit our ears and necks and left very itchy welts that persisted for many days. The last portage was the La Vase, which we reached on August 26; as the name implies, it is an extremely muddy portage. This portage led us to the La Vase River which flows into Lake Nipissing. From this point, the water flows in a westerly direction to Lake Huron.

Lake Nipissing is a sizable lake fifty miles long and fifteen miles wide. Our route followed the east shore where we found several native villages; these people are called the Nipissing but were called the Jugglers by the French explorers. As our brigade passed, men, women, and children came to the lake shore to watch us glide by with unconcealed curiosity. I later learned from the Ojibwe that the reputation of their shamans in casting spells makes them objects of fear and suspicion among the surrounding tribes. I traded for a few furs at one of the villages, and they seemed very pleased with my wares. This was the first time I saw the pelt of the caribou or reindeer which they called *adik*. They also showed me a shallow hollow in the rock that they said was made in olden times by the creator spirit *Nanabush* who made the hollow when sitting to rest at that spot to look over his work.

After paddling twenty-three miles down the east coast of Lake Nipissing, we came to and entered the French River which runs seventy miles downstream to Lake Huron. The river has many different channels of which four enter the lake. We followed the North or Voyager channel because an island near its mouth sheltered us from the waves of the big lake. We entered Lake Huron on the thirty-first of August, the passage up the Ottawa taking us twenty-seven days.

As we left the shelter of the rocky islands at the mouth of the French River, I began to feel the rhythmic rise and fall of our canoe in the incoming waves. At first, lake travel by canoe seemed perilous, but I soon saw that our craft, light, and buoyant rode the swells like a seabird. Our course was west and slightly north along the north shore of Lake Huron. Here, there is a channel between the Canadian mainland and the great Manitoulin Island which provided a calm passage. Before we entered the North Channel, however, we paused at La Cloche Island. This island takes its name from a large black basalt rock which, when struck, rings like a bell. I sought out this famous boulder and, indeed, did strike it. While it did ring, its tone was lower than the clear crisp sound we expect of a bell, yet it was a wonder still. La Cloche is inhabited by a band of Ojibwe who pass the summer months here in a large village.

Like many summer villages I encountered on my travels, I could smell this one before I could see it. Their odoriferous nature comes from several sources, offal from gutting fish and game animals left to rot in the sun, and the waste of several hundred people which accumulates on the outskirts of the village and to this must be added the strong but not altogether unpleasant smell of the pall of wood smoke and thousands of fish drying on racks.

I bartered some of my goods for dried fish and other meat, and they were friendly and hospitable to me until they learned that I was an Englishman. They then explained to M. Campion, who speaks some Ojibwe, that their kin at Michilimackinac would certainly kill me on sight and that, therefore, they had a right to share in the pillage of my possessions. Upon this principle, they asked for a keg of rum, saying that if I refused that, they would take it. I agreed when they gave their promise not to molest me further.

Now, after several dire warnings about my fate at the end of our journey, I was distressed and turned to Etienne Campion for advice. My first question was: "Why do the Indians treat me badly but are completely friendly with the French?"

After some thought, Etienne replied, "As you may know, the French and the Indians have been allies and trading partners for one hundred fifty years. During that time, we often lived among them and provided them with tools and other items which made their lives much easier. In fact, after all these years, they really would have a difficult time surviving at all without the goods we supply."

"Like what?" I asked. "They seem self-sufficient to me."

"There are many examples," said Etienne, "but by collecting furs, they trade for guns, powder, and shot to both feed and protect themselves from enemies. They get blankets to keep warm, brass and copper kettles for cooking and making maple sugar, and many implements such as iron axes, knives, hoes, and traps. All these items have changed their lives. They once made clay pots which were heavy and fragile, but now they use metal containers and have not made ceramic vessels in a hundred years.

"There is yet another important factor that binds the Canadians to the Indians," said Etienne. "Over all those years we have traded with the Indians, many Frenchmen have married Indian women and have produced generations of mixed blood children, the métis. The métis, of which there are now many in the Upper Country, are neither French nor Indians but are closely related to both. Moreover, they are very helpful to the Indians as advisors in their often difficult dealings with the French colonial government and the French military. Finally, most of the Indian traders are métis and therefore the very ones who actually provide the goods the Indians so desperately need."

"But what does all that have to do with hating the English? I have observed that I have many of the same goods for trade, and I hope you will not be offended if I observed that they are better made and cheaper than the ones traded by the French."

"Yes, I will admit that what you say is true, but the real problem is with the new trading policies of the English government. The English are afraid the Indians will use the firearms supplied by traders against their soldiers, so they have restricted the flow of guns, shot, and powder in the trade. To the Indians, this seems like an attempt to starve them and their families. Whereas the French gave the Indians many presents as token of goodwill. The English have restricted this practice because they regard giving presents as nothing but bribes. Besides these offensive policies, they resent the way they are treated by the English, which seems to them and, frankly to me, to be arrogant and patronizing."

"So what can I do, Etienne?" I asked.

"I have an idea, Alex. Perhaps we could disguise you as one of the voyagers until we get you inside Fort Michilimackinac. Perhaps it is already occupied by British soldiers, and they would surely protect you."

"If you think that would work, I will try. After all, I can't go back to Montréal."

"There are several problems in disguising you," said Etienne. "First, you don't speak much French. You're the only person in the upper country with such vivid blue eyes, and then of course there is your distinctive hair. These all make you an object of curiosity and attention."

"When you talk about my hair, I guess you are referring to my stripe?"

"But of course," he replied.

Here, I must mention that after my head was bashed open by the deserter villains along the Mohawk trail, my scalp gradually healed but with a large scar which ran from the base of my skull to the crown of my head. My hair is otherwise jet-black, but the new hair that grew on my scar is as white as snow.

"Do you really think the Indians will notice it?" I asked.

Etienne smiled broadly. "Have you noticed that the Indians have begun to call you *Zhigaag?*" he asked.

"Yes," I replied. "What does it mean? Do they think I am a female deity?"

"No, no, Monsieur, not a she—god."

"In their language, *zhigaag* means skunk."

"I guess they are referring to my hair?"

"In part," said Etienne, "but they also say all white men smell bad because we eat too many pigs, and after all, even among the French, we voyagers are known as '*mangeurs de lard*,' that is, pork eaters. You must understand, Alex, that in regard to the skunk name, Indians don't consider the various animals good or bad, just different from each other in particular ways just like people are different from each other. So calling you 'skunk' isn't a bad name."

"Certainly not the same way that calling me an Englishman is bad," I replied.

The next morning, with the amused help and clothing contributions from several of the voyagers, I was outfitted with the attire of the Canadian paddler consisting of a cloth passed around my middle, a loose shirt cinched with a woven sash, a molten or blanket coat, a large red scarf to be tied over my hair, and Indian moccasins. In this dress, I took my place among the paddlers.

It was not long before we passed several canoed loads of Indians who gave me no particular notice. We continued west of the North Channel passing many villages of Missisauga Ojibwe on the Canadian shore and an equal number of Amikouai Ojibwe on the north shore of Manitoulin Island. I was informed that the southern sandy shore of this island is a territory of the Odawa people.

We proceeded ever westward into a huge bay studded with many small islands which is called Potagannissing Bay. This bay is unimaginably beautiful. At a distance, the islets seem to float above the sunlit sparkling waters, while the sky, were it not for its soft white clouds, would be practically indistinguishable from the clear blue of the surrounding water.

We paddled south and saw a large Indian village located at the foot of a small bay near the middle of a large island called the Isle Odawa. We passed through the narrow De Tour passage into Lake Huron and followed the sandy island rich coast of Lake Huron to the west. The forest along this shore was a mixture maple, paper birch, and aspen as well as a component of spruce, fir, and cedar. As it is the beginning of September, the leaves were showing tints of yellow, orange, and red.

As we neared the Straits of Mackinac, we saw the smoke of numbers of Indian villages where the Indians were busy smoking trout and whitefish to preserve it for winter use. Entering the straits proper, we came to the island of Mackinac; its several plateaus rising above the lake gave the appearance of a huge turtle. In fact, I am informed that the Ojibwe word *mikinaak* means snapping turtle. In the legend of local Indians, Mackinac Island is the place where the earth was created.

As we passed close to Point Saint Ignace, the site of a former French fort and a Jesuit mission, we saw a substantial settlement at this place. A canoe filled with Indian men approached our brigade and asked if we had encountered any English in our travels. I was fearful of being discovered, but we were not detained. I did, however, see one of the Indians point at me with his chin and make a comment to his companion, and they both laughed. What he said I do not know, but they didn't seem to suspect me of being English.

From the north side of the straits, we could see smoke rising from the French settlement and fort on the south side, which is five miles distant across the water. We pointed our canoes in that direction and entered the straits. Here, we encountered fierce crosscurrents and high wind, which typically haunt these frigid waters for much of the year. In fact, the waves were so large that we were on the verge of throwing some of my *pieces* overboard in order to save our lives. Fortunately, as we approached the south shore, we were somewhat sheltered from the wind and encountered calmer water. The famous fort of Michilimackinac lay before us. Our trip from Montreal to Michilimackinac took somewhat less than two months. It was four o'clock in the afternoon, and my hopes for survival fell as I saw that the blue and gold *fleur de lis* flag of France still flew over the fort.

CHAPTER 6

S INCE IT WAS apparent that the British had not yet occupied the fort, we continued our subterfuge. M. Etienne Campion acted as the proprietor of our enterprise, and I remained in disguise. We landed our canoes at a small wharf located at the water-gate of the fort, which is indeed only a few yards from the water. The fort itself is enclosed by a palisade of twenty-foot sharpened cedar posts. Block houses commanded each corner, and an elevated walkway extended all around the interior of the curtain. Entering the water-gate, which is at the north side, I saw a storehouse and barracks immediately to the west and the quarters of the commandant to the east. A large parade ground dominates the interior east central interior, and a central street runs down the middle linking the water and land-gates. A large Jesuit church, a priest house, and a forge is to the west of the parade. Two row houses which are long, narrow dwellings divided into side-by-side apartments dominated the southern end of the fort, with the powder magazine occupying the southeast corner. The row houses are private dwellings, each with a small-fenced yard and a garden in the rear.

The architecture of the place is in the French style with buildings either of the *poteaux sur sole* or the *poteauxen terre* types in either case, upright timbers being chinked with mud. Roofs are steeply sloped and covered with cedar bark or with cedar shake shingles. The dwelling houses have an upper story containing a garret with window dormers. Each dwelling has a fireplace made of rounded beach cobbles and a chimney constructed by overlaid sticks with mud plastered in the interiors. The exterior of most of the dwellings is neatly plastered with mud. The row house apartments are the private homes of the fort's inhabitants that included several traders, retired French soldiers, and *métis* families. Children, chickens, pigs, and dogs roamed the fort grounds. By some standards, Michilimackinac would seem very rude; but to those of us who had recently endured the hard trip from

Montréal, it seemed the epitome of civilized life. Even the fort's stinking latrines seem a luxury.

M. Campion met with the acting commandant, the Ottawa *metis* war Chief Charles de Langlade, who was put in command of the fort when the French garrison, learning of the fall of Montréal, fled to the French-controlled Illinois country. Etienne readily secured housing and storage facilities for us, which had been made available by the departing French soldiers.

I'd no sooner settled into my lodging when I began getting visits from my new neighbors. Perhaps not surprising, given the chatty nature of the voyagers, they all seemed to know of my position and that I was an Englishman. In order to facilitate discourse with the inhabitants and the Indians, I employed as my translator a French trader, M. Farley, who spoke English and Ojibwe as well as French. From the inhabitants, I learned that my arrival had come to the attention of the local Ojibwe whose band chief was gathering his warriors to pay me a visit. They were brutally frank in telling me that I would soon be killed. For my part, I decided that my best allies in the fort were my own fortitude and patience.

At two o'clock the next afternoon, sixty Ojibwe approached my house. They were led by their chief, *Minavavana*. Walking solemnly in single file, they were naked to the waist, and their faces were painted black, while their chests and torsos were decorated with designs done in white clay. Some had feathers thrust through the septum of their noses, and others had their hair decorated with feathers. All carried a war ax in one hand and a knife in the other. The chief entered my house followed by the warriors who, on a sign from the chief, sat on the floor. *Minavavana* appeared to be about fifty years old and was six feet tall and of dignified and confident bearing. He studied me intently while he chatted with M. Campion through M. Farley. He remarked to them that I must be very brave to come among my enemies with so little fear. I kept up appearances with difficulty as I then believed that I was facing imminent death.

The Indians sat calmly and smoked a pipe as was their custom before getting down to business. When the pipe was finished, *Minavavana* drew out a narrow belt of wampum beads and begin to speak directly to me. It occurred to me that this council had been closely choreographed to indicate that it was an important event. *Minavavana* was a polished orator, and as I learned much later, he was not actually a chief but an *ogamagigido,* which is a special orator who speaks for his whole band on ceremonial occasions. I will not repeat in full all that he said to me, but I will attempt to convey its essence as it was imparted to me by M. Farley at a later time.

"Englishman," he said, "the Indians here are children of the French who have recruited them to make war on the English. Although the English have overcome the French king while he was napping, he will soon awake and call his children to destroy the English. Even though you have conquered the French Army, you have not conquered the Indians nor made peace with them. While making war for the French, many of our young men have been killed, and their spirits are unsatisfied. There are two ways to satisfy the spirits of the slain, either by avenging them by spilling the blood of the nation by which they fell or by 'covering the bodies of the dead.' That is done by making presents to allay the resentment of their relatives."

He then said to me that the English king had neither made peace with the Ojibwe nor covered their dead and that therefore they are still at war. He continued, "We see, however, that you are brave to venture among us and that you do not come to make war. We also see that you come to supply us with necessities that we much desire. Given this, we shall regard you as a brother, and you may sleep without fear of the Ojibwe." He then gave me a beautifully carved red stone pipe as a token of friendship. I reciprocated with the presents of tobacco and small iron tools which seemed to please them.

Minavavana then sat down and requested that his young men be permitted to taste the English milk, by which he meant rum. He said they were anxious to see how it compared with French milk. Given my misadventure after leaving Fort William Augustus, it made me tremble when Indians asked for ardent spirits. I did, however, promise to provide them a keg as a departing gift. Given the formality of this counsel, I felt obliged to now give my own reply speech. I first thanked the Ojibwe for their visit and noted that I came among them on the strength of their widespread reputation as men of good character and truthfulness. I said that they should now regard themselves as children of the English king who would furnish them with necessities. In conclusion, I said that their good treatment of me would encourage other English traders to come to them. They responded at many points of my talk by saying *"eh, eh"* which I am told is a sign of approbation among them.

Over the next few days, Etienne and I unpacked our goods, resorted their contents, and made up new *pieces*. We hired Canadian interpreters and clerks into whose care I would send the new *pieces* to the Indians living on *Michigami*, Green Bay, and Lake Superior and even to the far western country of the Sioux. Everything was ready for their departure when a new problem arose.

South and west along the *Michigami* shore, about thirty miles from the fort, is a large Odawa settlement called L'Arbre Croche which had strong ties of kinship and economy to Michilimackinac. Many of these Ottawa are Catholic and are engaged in growing corn, making smoked fish as well as a variety of manufactured items which they sell for the use of the many canoe brigades which originate at the fort. I am aware of their industry since I myself had purchased their dried corn to subsist my own brigades that were about to depart for a season of winter trading.

Last night at dusk, nearly two hundred Odawa warriors from L'Arbre Croche under the leadership of *Nisowaquet* or, as the Canadians knew him, La Fourche, arrived at the fort and ordered me and the two other Montréal traders, namely Stanley Goddard and Ezekiel Solomon, to counsel with them in the morning. I learned from Ezekiel that *Nisowaquet* was the maternal uncle and mentor to Charles de Langlade. Again, I will paraphrase the words of the chief who was an eloquent speaker.

"Englishmen," he said, "the Odawa see that you have brought many goods of which we are in great need. We are happy you have come, but now we see that you are preparing to send the same goods to other Indians. Some of these are our enemies. They will have your goods while our wives and children will be naked, cold, and hungry. Under these circumstances, we demand that you give each of our men ammunition, traps, and other merchandise in the amount of fifty beaver skins on credit which they will repay next summer."

We saw immediately that to comply with these demands would not only exhaust all our collective inventories, but we knew that these very Odawa had a reputation for not paying their credit debts. To make an impossible situation even worse, *Nisowaquet* said that since we had brought goods to their country without a peace treaty, they would take them if we did not give goods on credit. After this pronouncement,

Goddard, Solomon, and I armed ourselves and, along with some of our voyagers, spent the night guarding our stores while the Odawa held counsel among themselves. Despite our gloomy expectations, the night passed peacefully; and in the morning, we were surprised to find that every Odawa was gone from the fort. We soon learned that the reason for the departure was that the several hundred British redcoats who had been ordered to receive the surrender of the fort were only five miles away. We rejoiced and lost no time sending our trading brigades to the four winds.

Later that day, Capt. Henry Belfour led British troops of the Sixtieth and Eightieth Regiments as they marched into the fort, which was surrendered by Charles de Langlade. Captain Belfour, however, soon left Michilimackinac with most of his soldiers to occupy other former French posts. He did, however, order Lieutenant Leslie and forty men of the Sixtieth Loyal American Regiment to garrison this place.

During much of the rest of September and October, I spent my time preparing for the coming winter by gathering firewood and purchasing as much food as I could find. Most of the food available was dried corn and smoked fish that I acquired from Indian women in trade for blankets, woven goods, ribbons, and glass beads. Since some of my married voyagers had decided to over winter at the fort, I felt some responsibility to help them feed their families. As autumn wore on, everyone at the fort was busy collecting food and fuel which made these articles increasingly difficult to acquire. I heard, however, that apples, winter squash, and corn were available at a farm on French Farm Lake, which was only three miles southwest of the fort.

One bright and sunny day in October, I determined to visit French Farm Lake to see if I could get any fresher produce, and I set out along a trail leading in that direction. The day was warm, and occasionally a puffy wind gently tousled the golden poplar leaves. The sun shimmered through the huge old maple trees along the way, which had now turned bright shades of yellow and red. The whole scene produced elation, an undeniable impression that the very air around me had taken on these bright hues of fall. As I walked, I came upon a large grove of chestnut trees, the ground being so covered with the spiny husks of their nuts that walking was indeed difficult.

It was just then that I heard dogs shrilly barking and several shouts in the Indian language. I knew immediately from the tone of the voices that something was amiss. I went quickly toward the sounds and soon came to a small clearing where I found an Indian man and woman backed up against a huge chestnut trunk. A large basket of nuts was upset in the clearing and, most alarming, the bodies of two dead dogs. My attention was however fixed at the center of the clearing where a panther, sometimes called a lion or a catamount, was crouched. The tawny golden color of the cat almost concealed its form in the tall grass, but I could see that it was intently focused on the Indian couple. The man had no weapon, except for a knife, and the woman had armed herself with a stick, but neither weapon could be of any real use. The beast was low to the ground, its long tail straight behind and nervously twitching; its ears were laid back against its head, and its teeth were bared as it made harsh hissing sounds slowly stocking its prey. It moved so evenly that it almost seemed to float, yet I could see that its muscles were tense as coiled springs. Fortunately, the big cat did not see or scent my presence.

I raised my long rifle and steadied the barrel along a sapling. Aiming as the beast gathered itself for a final leap, I gently pulled the trigger. After a split second, the powder burned through the touch hole and ignited the barrel charge, and the ball flew through a dense cloud of gun smoke. As the smoke cleared, I saw the lion now lying still at the feet of the Indians. My ball had struck its skull just behind the ear, killing it instantly.

As I approached, the Indians were trembling and had slumped to a sitting position holding each other in shock. I began to examine the panther. It was a full-grown male and had a festering wound on one haunch. This infection had undoubtedly weakened the cat which probably accounted for its attack on humans.

Eventually, the man rose. He grasped my forearm and addressed me at length in his language. He was a man I judged to be about fifty years old, quite handsome, and very fit. He gestured to himself, repeating the word *Wawatum*, which I took to be his name. I, in turn, pointed to my own chest and said *Zhigaag*. They both nodded in understanding. *Wawatum* then put his hand on the shoulder of the woman, saying *Wabigonkwe*. She smiled shyly and then quickly and gently touched my face and then began to pick up the spilled chestnuts. Assured of their safety, I left them and continued to French Farm Lake where I found a large *métis* family from which I secured pumpkins, squash, and two bushels of dried corn.

CHAPTER 7

B Y LATE OCTOBER, the leaves had dropped and were scudding across the ground in brown waves in the face of a cold north wind. The days, so long in summer, grew shorter until by November. It was totally dark by the late afternoon. Increasingly, the sky was leaden, entirely composed of layers of clouds in every shade of gray. The fort grew quiet, except for the nervous calling of chickadees. There were now few Indians about as they had all scattered to their hunting territories for the winter; in short, life in all its forms was going into some form of hibernation.

The main activity of the men during this season, besides smoking before the fire, were hunting and fishing. Since most of big game has long been hunted to scarcity in the environs of the fort, there were few deer, elk, or moose to be found. I hunted the pure white snowshoe hare and red grouse, which are common in the frozen cedar swamps near the fort. For this purpose, I used an Indian trade musket loaded with small shot.

Owing to the fact that the water of the straits was rough and extremely cold during the late fall, fishing by the fort's occupants did not begin in earnest until the ice had formed in late December or early January. When the lake froze, the shoreline was clogged by huge jumbles of ice slabs pushed up by the motion of the water, while the lake was in the process of freezing. This mass had to be crossed to reach the flat frozen lake plain which stretched to the horizon in every direction. The ice is two or more feet thick, and where the snow cover is blown away, it is as clear as glass but for crisscrossed refrozen cracks and the occasional trapped air bubbles. As a novice to the ice, I was, at first, much concerned with the very loud cracking and grinding sounds the ice makes as it moves imperceptibly on the underlying water. The ice field is cold and extremely windy since there are no barriers to the stiff winds for almost one hundred miles across the unbroken surface. Falling and blowing snow often results in whiteouts which will cause complete disorientation to a fisherman caught on the ice. Besides an occasional human, any movement on the ice is the result of hungry opportunists such as foxes, crows, and ravens seeking tidbits of frozen fish.

There are two principal methods of fishing during the period of ice cover, both perfected by native people. The first is through the ice with gill nets. A line of small holes are first cut through the ice. A cord is then passed under the ice from hole to hole by means of a long pole. A large mesh net that has weights affixed to the bottom and floats attached to the top is tied to the line and then pulled under the ice from the first to the last hole; these are about three hundred feet apart. An anchor stone and a retrieval line attached to the net are sunk into deep water of perhaps one hundred feet or more. When fish, principally large whitefish, swim into the net, their heads pass through the mesh but cannot be withdrawn because the net catches their gill covers. Whitefish are in the lake in unimaginable numbers and, on the average, weigh between three and seven pounds. This species of fish, fresh or smoke-dried, are delicious and make up part of many winter meals for the fort's inhabitants. *Sagamity,* an Indian soup made from rehydrated corn and whitefish, is a highly nutritious and a very popular meal in these quarters.

The other fishing method is to take lake trout through the ice using a spear. These fish weigh ten to sixty pounds or more. Large holes are cut in the ice and covered with a dome made of branches which is, in turn, covered with skins or a blanket. The spearman slips under the dome on his belly and, in the darkness, can see clearly into deep water, perhaps to a depth of at least thirty feet. In one hand, he has a line attached to a wooden decoy carved to resemble a small whitefish which is the main prey of the trout. The decoy can be manipulated with the line to resemble a living fish. In the other hand, the fisherman holds a ten-foot spear. By moving the decoy from deep to more shallow water, he can gradually bring a hungry trout within the range of his spear. Baited hooks are also used with success for this species which is a vital winter food.

During the long winter evenings that I often spent in the company of Ezekiel, Solomon, and Stanley Goddard, I learned much about the geography and native people of the surrounding country. For example, I was told that the Indians of this area referred to themselves as *Anishnawbe,* which is best translated as "true human being." Implicit in this name is that people of other races, nationalities, or tribes, that is, people of separate creations, are less human than they themselves. Hearing the stories of these traveled and experienced traders, I became fascinated by their accounts of Sault Sainte Marie at the outlet of Lake Superior. This place, which they called the Sault, is only sixty miles as the crow flies north of Michilimackinac. To the Indians, the falls of the Saint Mary's River is known as *boweting,* and it is a location where very large numbers of Indians gather in the summer and fall to fish. It seemed to me like a good place for an Indian fur trader, so I resolved to visit the Sault in the spring.

I became particularly friendly with Ezekiel Solomon who I found to be a well-educated person with a great curiosity about his surroundings. His curiosity not only drew me to him, but I also realized it was a characteristic we shared. Ezekiel, who I often called Zek, was originally from the city of Berlin in Germany. He had immigrated to Montréal very recently and had nearly the same ambitions as myself. Unlike me, however, his entire family had been merchants for generations. Ezekiel was one of the first Jews to immigrate to Canada, and he told me he hoped to live at least part of each year in Montréal where a new Jewish congregation was taking root.

To look at him, one might get the impression that Ezekiel was a genteel scholar. He is a small man with black curls and a wispy beard. He wears small round eyeglasses which greatly magnify his eyes. He is always neatly dressed and prefers Eastern clothes to the leather garments and moccasins worn by his fellow traders. Zek is in fact a tough man who does not complain about hardship, who will pull his weight in any labor, and who knows how to drive a hard bargain. I thought it strange that he and I, who could not be from more different backgrounds, could end up on the same path in life.

My colleagues informed me that there is a resident trader at the Sault by the name of Jean-Baptiste Cadotte who is married to an Ojibwe woman by the name of Athanasius and that they have two sons; the elder son is called Jean-Baptiste, and the younger Michael. I am told they speak only Ojibwe in their home. By now, I was convinced that I must learn the language of my trading partners, and it occurred to me that if I could attach myself to the Cadotte household, I could learn their ancient and complex language.

CHARLES CLELAND

By early May, the ice finally retreated from the lakes; and on the first day of that month, I set out in a canoe for the Sault or *bowting* in the company of several Canadians. We passed eastward along the Lake Huron shore and entered the Detour passage where we headed north until we entered the Saint Mary's River which flows from the west. Several large islands lie in the lower reaches of this river, and much of the south shore is bordered with wet meadows. These are studded with patches of blue irises, as well as groves of pink lady slippers, which are in their splendor. At this season, the forest floor is a carpet of snow-white trillium and yellow trout lilies. Four days after leaving Fort Michilimackinac, we arrived at the small stockaded fort that the French called Fort Repentigny, which had originally been built to guard the entrance to Lake Superior.

This fort is located on the south bank of the Saint Mary's River about a half mile below the roaring rapids of the Sault. Here, the cold water of Lake Superior rushes, with white foam and mist over sandstone rubble which forms a twenty-foot drop to the Saint Mary's River below. The fort itself is the beginning of a rocky portage around the falls to the big lake beyond.

Inside the fort-picketed stockade are four buildings, the governor's house, the interpreter's house, and two small barracks buildings. M. Cadotte and his family occupied the interpreter's house where I also made arrangements to lodge. The other buildings are now vacant.

The Indians who reside permanently at the rapids are the Sault band of Ojibwe who are predominantly of the crane clan. This clan provides political leaders for the five Ojibwe bands who have their territories on the southeast end of Lake Superior and the Saint Mary's River valley. During the fishing season, which corresponds to the spawning time of the whitefish and lake trout which is roughly from September through mid-December, large numbers of Indians from the entire region gather at the rapids. Among those bands which regularly congregate here are members of the Nipissing, Amikwa, Marameg, Noquet, Mississauga, and Micmac bands as well as people of other small bands who are related culturally and in language to the local Ojibwe. After the fishing season, these bands dispersed to their distant territories.

No visitor to the Sault at this time of the year could resist a description of the remarkable and unique fishery that had been developed at that place. During spawning season, huge numbers of whitefish gather in the cold well-oxygenated water below and in the midst of the rapids. These are the same species of whitefish found in the lower lakes except larger—six to fifteen pounds—and I must say, in my opinion, tastier. In order to take these fish, two native men in a small canoe go into the swirling rapids, the one in the stern paddles and steers through the boiling water, while the other man stands in the bow with a scoop net that is attached to a ten-foot pole. The net man watches for concentrations of fish and thrusts his net into the school. His net seldom fails to come up filled with as many thrashing fish as it will hold. All this is accomplished without rolling these very light and unstable crafts. The whitefish are so numerous that even I managed to catch over five hundred fish with a scoop net that I dipped from rocks and small islets in the river.

During the fishing season, all the small Indian camps along the shore are engaged in making smoke-dried fish for winter use. To do this, the fish are gutted and tied together in pairs at the tail, and small sticks are inserted to keep the body cavity open. Many of these pairs of fish are then strung over a long pole. The pole is, in turn, suspended with others on a frame built over a low fire. The heat and smoke from the dripping fat dries and preserves the fish, which will provide the staple of the Indian's diet over the winter months. During this time, they will be engaged in hunting big game, which is often an unrewarding venture on a day in, day out basis.

During the summer, a small detachment of troops under the command of Ensign John Jamet arrived from Michilimackinac to garrison our fort. M. Cadotte and I were shocked to hear the new commandant's plan for provisioning his troops during the forthcoming winter. Being new to the country but deaf to advice, he planned to purchase a steady supply of venison from the Indians using the large store of liquor which was subject to his orders. Thankfully, this misbegotten scheme was never put to the test because of a very serious misfortune.

On the second day of December at one o'clock in the morning, I was awakened by loud and frightful shouts of "fire." I quickly dressed and ran out into the bitter cold and very windy night to find the fort ablaze. Parts of the stockade, the governor's house, and both barracks buildings were on fire. I soon learned that Ensign Jamet was still inside the governor's house, which was a raging furnace. Knowing the house, I rushed to his bedroom window and smashed it out, and thankfully, Jamet was able to escape by this exit. I also managed to save a small

CHARLES CLELAND

quantity of gunpowder from a barracks before the rest exploded. The fire destroyed the provisions of the troops and most of the food stores we had accumulated for winter use.

We were now under eminent threat of starvation and exposure to the elements, but fortunately, navigation was still open. The next morning, Ensign Jamet, who had joined me lodging in the Cadotte house, wasted no time and ordered the troops into canoes and sent them back to Michilimackinac; we later learned that they reached safety after a few days on the water. Several days later, the Saint Mary's River froze solid. As a result, we were cut off from Michilimackinac, having no way to reach the still unfrozen straits by boat.

During the course of these hard winter months, I got to know John Jamet quite well as we spent many evenings talking beside the fire, he being the only member of the household beside myself who spoke the English language with any degree of fluency. In the course of these conversations, I discovered that we had much in common. His father, like mine, had been a small landholder and farmer. He grew up in the English county of Kent and, like me, knew the hard life of a farmhand. But unlike my own case, he loved the farm and hoped to spend all his days as a farmer. Regretfully, however, his father died and left the farm to his elder brother who, because of his own large family, was not content to make a place for John. Suddenly at loose ends, seventeen years old, with no real home or means to earn a living, John enlisted as a soldier in His Majesty's infantry and was sent to fight the French and their Indian allies in North America. After ten years of hard service, he had been promoted to the rank of ensign; and as one of only three officers at Fort Michilimackinac, he hoped for a promotion to lieutenant.

After the fire, the few Canadians who had been living in a barracks found shelter with families in the metis community located nearby. We began to hunt and fish in earnest but with little success and soon became painfully aware that we must reach Michilimackinac to save ourselves. We waited until mid-February when we estimated that the Straits of Mackinac must be ice covered, thus permitting us to cross on foot. Our party, consisting of myself, Ensign Jamet, M. Cadotte, two Canadians, and two Indians, set out down the river on snowshoes. Our entire food supply for seven men consisted of some dried corn and fish, a little scorched pork, and a few loaves of bread which was made from partially burnt flour. Given that Jamet had never been on snowshoes, our progress was painfully slow and, in fact, disastrously slow, as it took us seven days just to reach Detour, the halfway point to the fort. It was still very difficult for me or any of us to be patient with Jamet. In my hunger and cold, I privately cursed him but would then think of my own first trip on snowshoes along the frozen Saint Lawrence. I now know how my guide M. Bodoine felt, and this knowledge tempered my impatience with Jamet. After a brief feeling of charity, I imagined a very drunk Bodoine leaving his warm fire and his drunken Indian companions to chase me through the dark, cold woods in the middle of the night. That thought brought a smile to my face even under the stress of present conditions. We determined that our best option was to send the Canadians and Indians who could move fast on snowshoes back to the Sault for more food. This was a ninety-mile round trip, and they returned four days later with a small amount of corn and dried meat. We immediately headed west along the north coast of Lake Huron which was heavily forested with cedars. After three days of short marches, Ensign Jamet could not continue as his feet were severely blistered from the rubbing of his snowshoe bindings. We were again in dire need of food and had progressed too far to return to the Sault, and we were not even sure how far it was to our destination. After much discussion, we decided that our best hope was for me and one of the Canadians to go as fast as possible to Fort Michilimackinac for help. We set off the next morning at sunrise, and by midmorning, we could see columns of smoke rising to great heights in the cold air to our far west. We reached the fort later in the afternoon of the next day, and a rescue party soon brought in the rest of our company.

In my absence, the fort had come under the command of Major Etherington of the Sixteenth Regiment who arrived from Detroit in the summer with a garrison force of thirty-five soldiers. In only a short time, I had reason to judge Etherington to be both arrogant and overconfident, a combination which can be disastrous for someone who was entirely new to the far frontier of the British Empire.

I decided for various reasons to return to the Sault as soon as possible, but during my brief residence at the fort, there was a personal event which, out of modesty, I'm most reluctant to mention and would not, except for the fact that this episode played an important part in saving my life during the following summer.

As will perhaps be recalled, my mother died while I was quite young, and I was raised by my father in a womanless household. Through my teen years, I had almost no contact with the opposite gender. At school, I was attracted to several of my female classmates, but I did not understand these feelings, and I was not informed of the basic facts of life over and above what I knew from my own observation of our farm animals. My father was not one to talk of intimate details or to tell risqué jokes. In fact, he never used rough language and often said that he preferred to totally avoid what he called the Anglo-Saxon words, preferring those more polite forms that were the legacy of the Norman Conquest. As a result of this sheltered upbringing, I was never comfortable in the company of young women as I felt shy and uneasy in their presence. Once I began my travels, I occasionally came into contact with tavern girls and camp followers. I found myself shocked and embarrassed by their forward suggestions which I did not really understand. Although I did learn some of the basic facts of romantic engagement, I had never become physically involved with any woman. During my time in the company of soldiers and voyagers, both breeds of which seemed to talk incessantly about their conquests both real and imagined, I'm ashamed to say that I pretended relationships with women that I did not, in fact, experience. This being the case, I was not able to ask any pertinent questions of these experienced men.

One night as I was sleeping in the garret of the house of fellow trader Stanley Goddard where I was temporarily lodged, I came awake realizing that someone else was in my bed. At first, I thought it was a drunken voyager who had mistakenly climbed the wrong ladder and ended in my bedchamber; but upon some further explorations, I was shocked to find that the person in bed beside me was a totally naked woman. Her warm, soft body was against me, and as I stirred, she began to sing softly into my ear, and her hands began to move over my body, and I soon became aroused beyond all rational control. I let my own desires loose upon her, and as I explored her body, she began to breathe quickly and move against me and to purr with pleasure. My ability and need to please her only fueled my desire, and perhaps sensing my inexperience, she led us, and together we surged through wave after wave of exquisite passion. I will here leave out many startling and enjoyable details.

As we eventually lay exhausted and holding each other, I lit a candle and, in the light, caught the first glimpse of my paramour. She was a small and well-proportioned Indian woman, perhaps of my own age. She had very long black hair which smelled of wintergreen. Her eyes were likewise very dark, and they shone with wit and intelligence. Her complexion was slightly scarred from smallpox, and her back had a web of-old scars, left by beatings. However gentle her touch, her hands were calloused by hard work.

As best as we could, we managed to communicate in a mixture of French and Ojibwe; although at this time, we both spoke these languages poorly. I learned that her name was Josette and that she was a *pani*, that is, an Indian slave. She told me she was of the Degiha people and a member of the Ponca tribe. She was born and raised in small village along a river called the Niobrara near where it enters the Missouri River. Her people lived on the long grass prairies where they hunted buffalo and planted their gardens. As a girl, Josette, who was then called *Nuge* or Summer in the Ponca language, helped her mother with every kind of work but most enjoyed using her digging stick to harvest wild potatoes. One early morning, when she was twelve summers old, she was engaged in just this activity with her young friends when a raiding party of Illini Indians swept down upon her small village. Josette was among those captured by this band of slavers and carried off across the Mississippi River.

On the other side of this mighty river, she was taken to a Peoria Indian village where she became a *pani* or slave and was attached to the household of one of the leaders of the raiding party. She remained in this house for several years where she endured frequent beatings by the wife who often thrashed her with a rawhide quirt.

Eventually, Josette was sold to French trader named La Vake who took her to Fort Saint Joseph at the southern end of Lake *Michigami*. It was here that she was given the name Josette, and she began to learn to speak the French language. She was also forced to spend her days skinning animals and curing their hides. Her French master loved rum and high wine, and when he was drunk, which was often, he abused her. She told me that two years ago, La Vake took her with him on a trading trip to the Michilimackinac rendezvous. Here, La Vake lost her in an Indian gambling game to M. de Langlade; and hence, she became a *pani* in his home. The de Langlades treated her kindly, but she longed for the day when she might be free to come and go as she pleased.

She told me that she had watched me many times as she was working around the de Langlade household and judged me to be a good man who appealed to her as a lover. She had rightly judged my shyness with women and decided to come to me as she had, fearing I would never approach her. Although Josette appeared frequently in my dreams thereafter, I, nevertheless, soon left the fort to return to the Sault.

CHAPTER 8

I WAS DETERMINED to be back at Michilimackinac when my *engagees* returned from their various wintering grounds so that I could collect their furs and prepare them to be sent on to Montréal. My partner, M. Etienne Campion, who had returned to Montreal with a canoe brigade in the fall, would take care of our business arrangements involving the sale of our pelts and the resupply and shipment of new trade goods to me here at Michilimackinac. With these intentions, I left the Sault in late April and, with two Indian guides, traveled the overland trail south to Saint Ignace on the north side of the Straits of Mackinac, a journey of four days. By that time, most of the snow was gone from the woods, except for patches in the deep shade. Here, the heat from the spring sun absorbed by the wet black trunks of the hardwoods caused the snow to melt around the trunks, making it appear as though the trees were growing from holes. At Saint Ignace, I borrowed a small canoe, and we proceeded to paddle across the straits. It was a cool day on the water, but the warm sun shining in a pale blue sky, as well as a slight breeze, made the air itself seemed light.

As I approached the fort, I immediately perceived a major change since I had left the place the previous fall. The beach and area around the fort were filled with hundreds of dome-shaped Indian dwellings, or *waakaiigan,* as well as many canoes. In fact, the whole scene was a beehive of activity. I estimated that no fewer than three hundred Indians were camped around the fort. In addition, there were also hundreds of Canadians voyagers walking about and many thirty-foot freight canoes drawn up on the beach, indications that many of the Canadian *engagees* had already returned. Since the wharf and area around the water-gate were crowded with men unloading and loading canoes, I made landfall to the east of the fort on the northernmost point of land.

Making my way toward the land-gate, I was aware that the Indians who would usually greet me with friendly calls of *boozhoo* or *aaniin* were silent and sullen. I recognized very few of them, and many seemed to be from strange tribes and places. I soon made my way to the row house dwelling I had rented next door to the one occupied by Charles de Langlade and his family. At this time, there were three other English traders living in the fort beside myself, namely Ezekiel Solomon, Henry Bostwick, and Mr. Tracy, whose first name I have long since forgotten. The fort's garrison consists of Major Etherington, Lieutenants Leslie and Jamet, and thirty-five privates.

No sooner had I settled than I was visited by my old friends Solomon and Bostwick who regaled me with dire rumors of Indian unrest. Henry Bostwick in fact was accompanied by a Canadian trader, M. Laurent Ducharme, who had recently arrived from the Detroit area. M. Ducharme related a disturbing story which he had learned from his friends among the southern Odawa.

"What do you hear, Monsieur?" I asked.

"Well, my friends, there is an Odawa war chief in the south by the name of Pontiac who is very talented as a leader and military strategist. Pontiac has managed to put together a confederacy of tribes in the Ohio Valley and Great Lakes area that is dedicated to driving the English from all the country west of the Allegheny Mountains."

"But how could he take all the British forts with their cannons and well-trained soldiers?" Bostwick asked.

"It is said that Pontiac has magical powers bestowed by the teachings of a Delaware prophet and that he can take the British posts by guile."

"Do you believe this is possible, M. Ducharme?" Ducharme reflected on my question for a moment and frowned before replying.

"It makes no difference what I believe, Messieurs," he said with a shrug. "Pontiac's Pottawatomie, Illinois, Miami, Ottawa, and Ojibway warriors firmly believe it, and there are at least five hundred warriors representing these tribes now gathered around Detroit."

"But what about Fort Michilimackinac?" I asked.

"Well," Ducharme replied, "the local Ojibwe war chief *Machekiewis* is a follower of Pontiac, and he has received wampum war belts from Pontiac, so I believe he is committed to making trouble here."

"Did you tell Major Etherington about this?" Solomon asked.

"Oh yes, the day I arrived from Detroit, but that horse's ass called me a coward and said that if I repeated my lies, he would send me to Detroit in chains."

On the seventeenth day of May, I was visited by my friend *Wawatum* and his wife *Wabigonkwe* who had just returned from their winter hunt. It may be remembered that I saved this couple from a panther in the fall of 1762. By now, thanks to my stay with the Cadotte family in the Sault, I could carry on an ordinary conversation in the Ojibwe–Odawa language, but I must say that the tongue is so extravagantly figurative, that it takes a perfect mastery to truly comprehend its meaning. At any rate, *Wawatum* told a story, and as clearly as I could perceive it, given my language skills, it is as follows: As a young man, after observing a long fast and mortification of his body, *Wawatum* experienced a vision whereby he, as an older man, adopted an Englishman as a son and a friend. He told me that when he saw me emerge from the trees after I killed the panther, he immediately recognized me as the person he had seen many years before in his youthful vision. *Wabigonkwe,* whose name means Flower Woman, then presented me with the hide of the panther that she had beautifully tanned and tailored to be worn as a cape. In accepting this gift, I also formalized the relationship *Wawatum* had described in his vision, and he became my *noss,* or father, and I became his son, or *ningozis*, while *Wabigonkwe* became my *ninga,* or mother.

After these formalities were completed, *Wawatum* told me in no uncertain terms that he was sad that I had returned from the Sault and that I should go back there perhaps as early as tomorrow. He then asked me if the English warrior chief at the fort had heard any gossip or bad news or as he put it, "The singing of bad birds." He told me also that there were many Indians in the neighborhood of the fort who had not shown themselves. Although *Wawatum's* hints of impending danger were obvious to me later, they seemed so vague at the time that I was oblivious to their true meaning.

A few mornings later, *Wawatum* again appeared at my house, this time with his entire immediate family which included besides his wife, *Wabigonkwe*, his son, *Miskomiigwan* or Red Feather, and his son's wife, *Anangons* or Little Star. *Miskomiigwan* or simply Feather, *Miigwan*, as he was known to his family, was about thirty years old; he had a pleasant open face and intelligent eyes. With a quick smile, he grabbed my forearm and called me *nishiime* or younger brother. His wife, *Anangons,* was about twenty years old and very pregnant. She was also an exceedingly beautiful woman. Like her husband, she had a quick and inviting smile. Her dark eyes seemed to sparkle, and she had a long nose which somehow added to her appealing beauty. As the wife of my brother, *Anangons* was my *niinim* or sibling-in-law of the opposite sex. As I was to learn over the next many months, each of these new kin terms had special and different expectations for me and of me. These included a set of complex obligations and special rules of etiquette related to each relationship that were very important in maintaining peace and security within the family, indeed important for the very survival of the family of which I was now a member.

After introducing my new relatives, *Wawatum* and *Wabigonkwe* presented me with a huge and very valuable gift consisting of many furs, items of Indian clothing, sleeping robes, snowshoes, and much dried meat and fish. This gift required that I make one of equal generosity, and I provided *Wawatum* and *Miigwan* with guns, powder, and shot (contrary to British Indian trade policy) as well as knives, a spyglass, and many silver armbands. For *Wabigonkwe* and *Anangons,* I gifted brass kettles, axes, hide scrapers, blankets, ribbons, and yards of cloth, needles, awls, and clasp knives. With this exchange, we sealed our new relationship. My new father now began to try to persuade me in the most earnest terms to leave Michilimackinac as soon as possible. I explained, however, that my trade business required my presence here until the late summer. As I made this declaration, I was astonished to see tears stream down the cheeks of both *Wawatum* and *Wabigonkwe,* and they left me.

The days of late May passed quickly, but although I traded a few knives and axes to the many Indians who came to my trading counter, business was unaccountably slow. While many potential customers carefully examined my goods and particularly silver items, they did not seem interested in parting with their furs in exchange. It would not be long before the reason for this strange behavior revealed itself.

The morning of June 2, 1763, was clear and bright; and as we had been informed on the previous day, the local Ojibwe were to play a game of *baggatiway* which the Canadians call *le jeu du la crosse,* against a team of visiting Sauk Indians. This game is very amusing as it involves many scores of players on each team with the object being to throw a ball to a goal using a four-foot stick with a small rawhide basket attached to the end. The ball is passed from player to player by means of this racket in order to advance it toward the team's goal. In the process, opposing players try to intercept the ball and to move it in the opposite direction.

This struggle leads to much violence as the players surge this way and that often using their rackets to create mayhem on the bodies of their opponents. The game was to take place just outside of the fort with one goal being near the palisade. The Indians, who are invariant gamblers, wagered enormous amounts on the outcome of the game.

I did not plan to see the game as I was trying to untangle some problems with my account books. So when I was interrupted by Mr. Tracy who dropped by to see if I would care to accompany him to watch the game in the company of the officers, traders and soldiers who were not on duty in the fort. I declined Mr. Tracy's offer, a decision which surely saved my life. Mr. Tracy left my house and had not gone twenty paces from my door when I heard an Indian war cry and much shouting. Advancing to my window, I saw a crowd of Indians rushing into the fort and spreading out to cut down and scalp every Englishman they could lay their hands on. I had a gun loaded with swan shot, and I waited to hear the army's drumbeat to arms, which regretfully never came. I was horrified to see my friend Lieutenant Jamet with sword in hand facing off against a half-dozen Ojibwe warriors. He was slashing and thrusting and afflicting some serious wounds on his attackers who were circling him and darting in to slice with their knives and war axes. Jamet gave ground until his back was against a wall where he could better ward off those assaulting him. One of the Indians hurled a spear which struck Jamet in the thigh and knocked him to the ground. The warriors, apparently enraged by his stout defense, now pounced on him like a pack of wolves. They slashed and stabbed him with knives and chopped with their axes until poor John was reduced to a pile of gore. His attackers scooped up handfuls of his blood which they drank and smeared on their bodies. I gagged and vomited at the horror of it all.

As if seeing my friend John defiled in such a manner was not terrifying enough, an instant later, I saw Mr. Tracy, not thirty feet from my window, struggling between the knees of a large Indian who was busy scalping him while he was still alive. He too died in the assault.

Hearing no drumbeat calling us to arms and seeing no resistance from the many Canadians who stood by watching the slaughter, I quickly concluded that armed resistance on my part would be of no avail against the many rampaging warriors. I knew my only hope was to hide. There being a door to my side yard which abutted the house of M. de Langlade, I waited my chance and quickly darted across my garden,

CHARLES CLELAND

jumping the fence and crawling to the back door of the de Langlade dwelling. I entered and found the family watching the attack from their windows, which like mine overlook the Rue Dauphin where much of the carnage was taking place. I addressed myself to M. de Langlade asking that he preserve me from the massacre, but while I appealed to him, he turned back to the window and, with a shrug, said he could do nothing for me.

At that moment, I felt a tug of my elbow and turned to find my friend Josette, the *pani* woman who was a servant in the household. She beckoned me to follow her, and she led me to a stairway which led to a garret with a locked door. She produced a key and bade me to enter and then locked it behind me. The room was dark, and apart from an old mattress on the floor and a huge pile of baskets in one corner, it was entirely empty. I discovered that the floorboards of the garret were also the ceiling boards of the room below, so I could hear and see all that transpired there through the cracks. I also found a small gap between the cedar shakes which made up the slanting roof of the house, and from there, I could observe the foul activities taking place outside. Dead and dying soldiers were scattered about, and Indian men and women were busy scalping and mutilating their remains. The scene was terrifying, and as I watched, I unconsciously intertwined my fingers and found myself clasping my hands together with such force that I could feel my own pulse beating as if I held my own living heart in my hands. My whole body was shaking in horror and fear. As I watched, the killing frenzy at last began to abate, and I saw a group of prisoners being roughly escorted toward the water-gate. I was somewhat relieved to see Zek Solomon and Henry Bostwick among the soldiers that composed the majority of the captives.

It was not long before a group of blood-soaked warriors entered the de Langlade house. I observed them through the floorboards as they asked M. de Langlade if any Englishmen were in the house. De Langlade replied that "he could not say" which was true since I had been hidden without his knowledge. The Indians then asked to examine the garret. While the locked door caused a delay in their search, I seized the opportunity to bury myself under the pile of baskets. Having hardly secured my hiding place, the door was unlocked, and the searchers entered. Fortunately, the room was dark; and although they passed so close to me that I could have touched their moccasined feet, they did not discover my hiding place. Presently they passed down the stairs, and the door was relocked.

With the danger passed, I lay down on the mattress and eventually fell into an uneasy sleep. I was awakened later in the afternoon by Madam de Langlade who had come to the garret to patch a leak in the roof. She was alarmed to find me, but regaining her composure, she advised me to remain hidden as the Indians had killed most of the English and would not hesitate to kill me. I begged her to send me some water, and in the evening, my *pani* friend came with water and dried meat. Her ministrations to me included soothing and hopeful words, as well as soft caresses. Although comforted, my dire situation would not permit amorous feelings on my part.

In the morning, Indians again entered the de Langlade household; and as I listened, I heard my Indian name *Zhigaag* mentioned, and I surmised that they were telling de Langlade that I was not among the prisoners nor had my body been found among the dead. They asked him again if he was hiding me in his house and told him that if I was there, and he did not surrender me, that they would extract revenge on his children. This pronouncement sent Madame de Langlade into hysterics, and she told her husband, using the French tongue, that it was better I should die than they. De Langlade, who by now knew of my presence, led the warriors up the stairs; and there being no point in my hiding, I presented myself in full view.

One of the warriors, who was painted black from head to toe, except for two white spots around his eyes, quickly stepped forward, roughly grabbed me, and claimed me as his personal prisoner. Despite his war paint, I recognized him as a former customer by the name of *Wenniway*. We had had a violent dispute the previous fall when I refused him credits, and I feared that he was now bent upon revenge. *Wenniway* grabbed me by the collar and, banishing a large butcher knife, held it to my neck. I trembled violently, believing I would be killed on the spot. He stared into my eyes for a long time and then declared he would be adopting me to replace a brother who had been lost fighting the English. He took me downstairs with the intention of taking me to his lodge in the Indian settlement. I knew that in ransacking the fort, the Indians had discovered stores of rum and that most were by now very drunk. I doubted I would survive long in their midst and voiced this opinion to M. de Langlade who, in turn, appealed to *Wenniway* to leave me in his care for the present. To this, he consented but came back to claim me within the hour, now obviously drunk himself. He ordered me outside and insisted we exchange clothing, and he then led me away from the fort toward a patch of woods and high sand dunes to the west. I now perceived that he had changed his mind about adopting me and was preparing to cut my throat. Insisting on changing clothes would assure that my attire, which he coveted, would not be ruined by my blood. With this belief in mind, I refused to go any further.

Wenniway had a rather short and powerful body typical of many Ojibwe males, and he was stronger than I was by far.

As I balked, I said, "You are going to kill me. I can see it in your eyes, you are a liar. You never intended to adopt me. You are going to kill me for my clothes."

Wenniway said, "Yes, you are right. You are a cheating trader, and you are about to die."

Now I again turned to my early training in fisticuffs. As he raised his knife, I brought my right fist up in a vicious uppercut. The punch landed on the point of his chin, and he staggered, dropping his knife, and I wrenched free of his grip. I ran back to the fort as fast as I could, but *Wenniway* soon followed. Seeing M. de Langlade's door opened, I ran in; and for whatever reason, my captor did not follow.

I then returned to the garret and, after a time, slept in utter exhaustion. At some point in the evening, I was aroused by Josette and summoned to a meeting downstairs. To my great surprise, I found Major Etherington, Lieutenant Leslie, and Henry Bostwick waiting for me. They told me that the Indians, apparently wishing to devote the night to drinking rum and celebrating, had left all the prisoners in the fort under the care of the Canadians. Thus, although whites were in actual possession of the fort at this time, the Indians, who were all outside of the palisade, controlled it.

Given our short reprieve, we took the opportunity to discuss our situation. Major Etherington recounted how the *baggatiway* players had thrown the ball over the palisade and swarmed through the land-gate in its pursuit. As they ran past the crowd of spectators, Indian women pulled weapons from under their blankets and passed them to the warriors entering the fort. The soldiers of the garrison, many of them spectators themselves, were taken totally by surprise, and there was no meaningful resistance. As far as the major could calculate, sixteen privates and Lieutenant Jamet had been killed outright, with two privates seriously wounded. Mr. Tracy was also killed. That left, besides himself, about twenty privates, Leslie, three traders, including myself, and an English visitor from Detroit in captivity. He believed that some of us would also be killed before dawn.

We also speculated about the motives for the attack, and it was very plain that it had no racial motivation, since despite the war frenzy, which had taken English lives, no white Canadians were hurt or their property damaged. We also discussed the prospects of closing the gates of the fort and trying to defend it against the Indians outside. We concluded, however, that with insufficient arms and men, no help from the Canadians, opposition of the parish priest, Fr. Du Jaunay, and no possibility of military relief for months that we had no realistic chance of armed resistance.

In the morning, a party of Indians, including a sullen *Wenniway* with a badly swollen jaw, came to the de Langlade house and took me away to a small room in the King's storehouse where Mr. Solomon, the English visitor from Detroit, and a redcoat private were being held. The four of us were soon taken to the beach where a canoe was being readied. It was very cold, and I had on only a thin cotton shirt; I was shivering uncontrollably when a Canadian bystander gave me his blanket. Were it not for his act of kindness, I could not have endured the journey that followed.

As we departed under the escort of two Indian warriors, we were told that we were to be taken to the *Isle du Castors*, or Beaver Island, a large island in Northern *Michigami*, and turned over to the local Ojibwe. There was no doubt in any of our minds that we would be killed.

About eighteen miles west of Fort Michilimackinac is a low sandy peninsula of the mainland, which terminates in a large number of islets separated from each other by shallow water. This peninsula is known as *Waagoshense* or Red Fox Point. To avoid going around this point, canoes passing from the Straits of Mackinac south along the east coast of *Michigami* must take passage between its islands. This course brought us into Sturgeon Bay just as a dense fog blew in from *Michigami*, forcing us to closely follow the shore of the mainland. This route also brought us close to Odawa villages such as La Crosse and L'Arbre Croche. To our surprise, an Indian man appeared out of the fog on the beach and shouted at us inquiring about the news. We slowed and drew near to the shore as our escorts engaged him in conversation. Suddenly a shout was heard, and about one hundred Odawa warriors bounded out of the dunes into the water and seized our canoe. Fate had yet again intervened to change our destiny; we did not know if for the better or worse.

CHAPTER 9

N O SOONER WERE we captives in the hands of the Odawa than we were approached by their chiefs. As Ojibwe and Odawa tongues are but dialects of the same language, I was able to communicate with little difficulty. I did notice, however, some smiles and, in several cases, outright laughter at my choice of words and my Ojibwe pronunciation. The chiefs told us that we were now prisoners of the Odawa who had just saved us from being "made into broth" by the Ojibwe on Beaver Island. The chiefs said that the Odawa were traders like ourselves and had few complaints about the English who carried better goods to them than the French. They also expressed their outrage that the Ojibwe would attack the fort without consulting their Odawa brothers. These complaints about Ojibwe behavior made us feel we were in better hands, but in the end, we were still prisoners. The Odawa then loaded us into canoes, and accompanied by at least one hundred warriors, we set out to return to Fort Michilimackinac where we arrived in the early evening. As we were marched into the fort, now in the possession of the Odawa, the events of the last few days seemed more like a dream than reality, more like fiction than the truth. The Odawa quickly escorted the four of us to the commandant's house where we were held under tight guard.

Early the next morning, the Odawa and Ojibwe held counsel to voice their differences. The Ojibwe complained that the Odawa had stolen their prisoners and then claimed that the Odawa were the only Indians that did not follow Pontiac. They further contended that the French king had awakened from his nap and that Pontiac and his allies had taken all the British forts west of the mountains, except Detroit which was under siege. They asked the Odawa to restore their prisoners and to join the war on the English. The council was then adjourned until the next day to give the Odawa time to discuss the situation among themselves. When the council resumed the following day, we were totally dismayed and frightened when the Odawa agreed to return us to the Ojibwe.

As soon as we were restored to them, the Ojibwe marched us to their nearby settlement where we were interred in a prison lodge where fourteen bound soldiers were being kept. At noon, *Menehweha*, along with *Wenniway*, entered the prison lodge and seated themselves at the far end. To my surprise, *Wawatum* suddenly appeared and joined the other two; I had often wondered during the last few days what had become of him. These three sat and smoked in utter silence, and then *Wawatum* got up and left, saying to me as he passed by, "Have courage."

Other Indians began entering the lodge over the next hour as if preparing for a counsel, and at length, *Wawatum* and *Wabigonkwe* entered, carrying many goods, which they piled in front of *Menehweha* and *Wenniway*. In due time, *Wawatum* rose and began to speak. Addressing the chief, he reminded them that they all had sons, brothers, wives and daughters—family that they loved. He also reminded them that he had such a family and that he had adopted me as a son into his family. Now that son sat before them as a slave. As his son, *Wawatum*, told them, I was also a relative of theirs and as such, how he asked, could they make their own relative a slave at the same time? He then noted that when the attack on the fort started, the chiefs, fearing that he might inform me of their plans, had asked him to leave Michilimackinac until after the hostilities. He had done this, he said, in exchange for the promise that I would not be endangered during the attack. *Wawatum* now said that he had come to claim me but that he had not come empty-handed, indicating the pile of presents.

Menehwehna then replied that all that *Wawatum* had said was true and that everyone had been good to his word. He concluded by saying, "I am very glad that your friend has escaped. We accept your presents, and you may take him home with you." *Wawatum* thanked the speaker and took me by the hand and led me to his lodge which was only a few yards from the prisoner's lodge where the council was being held. Needless to say, I was overjoyed at my good fortune. I found myself as one of the family and was served the first hearty meal since my captivity.

In the morning, I awoke to much noise coming from the prisoner's lodge; and looking out the door, I saw the bodies of five soldiers being dragged out of the place of my own recent captivity. Shortly later, two Indians cut up a dead soldier, putting the dismembered parts into five large kettles hanging over fires. That evening, there was to be the warrior's victory celebration to which *Wawatum* was included. After a short time at the celebration, he returned to our lodge with a steaming bowl of soup which he sipped but did not appear to relish. *Wawatum* offered it to me, and as I reached to take the bowl, I noticed that it contained part of a human hand and a lump of flesh. Seeing my horror, *Wawatum* explained, "It is the custom of the Indians to celebrate a victory over enemies by making a feast of the slain. This inspires the warriors to attack and breeds him to face death with fearlessness."

I was utterly outraged and sickened by this barbaric ritual and claimed that they were nothing but savage cannibals. My horror was deepened by the fact that I thought I recognized the hand as belonging to my friend Jamet. In hindsight, however, I concluded that this was a delusion on my part created by my deranged mind in a moment of revulsion and terror. I raged on for a time, berating *Wawatum* and the Ojibwe in general for an ungodly practice. *Wawatum* remained calm until I regained control of my wits, but he was not without a rejoinder. "We eat only our brave enemies," he said, "since consuming part of them confers on us their bravery and skill in combat. Our warriors did consume some meat of the redcoat with the long knife, whom you called Jamet because he was the bravest of the redcoats. It is said that he faced fifty of our men in combat, that he killed many and slashed many more. He spilled much blood, and our warriors drank his blood out of respect and admiration. We do know cannibalism, but this is not such. I hope you never meet the *Windigo*, the cannibal giant of the dark winter woods."

Wawatum was not finished here. "How," he asked, "does this eating differ from the one so frequently done by the black robe witch, who the whites call priest and who talks in the big lodge with the cross? He uses magic to make the meat and blood of their god which they also eat so as to take on his spirit. I have myself seen this eating of the body and blood, and I ask you, is not this just as we do?"

"Yes," I said. "In some ways, it is similar, but the priest doesn't kill men to get the meat and blood. It is only a symbol."

"This is so," said *Wawatum*, "but the priest only tells a story, while we eat the real meat and blood. Is it not a more direct way to give these brave enemies a new life?"

CHARLES CLELAND

With this exchange, our theological debate came to an unsatisfactory end. As a footnote, I learned later that the prisoners not killed at this time all survived. My friends, Zek Solomon and Henry Bostwick, and the officers, Etherington and Leslie, were taken to Montréal by the Odawa and ransomed. Others, including surviving soldiers from Fort Michilimackinac and some of the other posts taken by Pontiac's warriors, were later released or ransomed. Because Detroit could be supplied by water, Pontiac's long siege was stymied, and the fort remained in British hands.

During the weeks and months after the fall of Michilimackinac, the local Indians lived in increasing fear that the British Army would descend upon them to extract an awful vengeance. After all, such a result would surely have occurred in the context of their own tribal warfare. Fearing immediate retribution, the assembled Indians decided to move to Mackinac Island because it could be more easily defended. Accordingly, packing began; and by the next morning, a steady stream of canoes was headed for the island, including myself in company with the *Wawatum* family.

Mackinac Island rests at the junction of Lakes *Michigami* and Huron, and it holds a central place in Indian mythology, history, and economy. The island is home to a *metis* band made up principally of Canadian voyagers and Indian women of both Ojibwe and Odawa descent. Since the men are gone much of the year, the resident population is mostly made up of women and mixed blood children.

Our canoe landed in the small harbor on the southeast side of the island where a flat meadow studded with red and yellow hawkweed flowers offered ample room for our many lodges. Behind the meadow rises a forty-foot vertical limestone cliff. A path leads to these higher elevations, which are covered with huge cedars, pines, and spruce trees with maples and birches dominating on yet a higher ridge. From these vantage points, one can see the Straits of Mackinac to the west and two large islands to the south and east. The water from these heights is a beautiful sapphire blue as it sparkles under the summer sun.

It took our women, *Wabigonkwe* and *Anangons*, only a short while to set up our lodge made of reed mats and sheets of birch bark placed on a frame that was made of newly cut poplar saplings bent and tied to form a dome about ten to twelve feet in diameter. An opening at the top to permits smoke to escape, and a deer skin covers the door opening.

Beds of cedar boughs covered with skins and sleeping robes were made along the walls, and in the center, a small fire was kindled for cooking and warmth. Our whole family could be accommodated in this small space, as none but I seemed to mind close quarters.

When the exodus from Michilimackinac was complete, there were about three hundred Ojibwe warriors in our camp, a very serious military force among these people. *Wawatum* told me, however, that a food scarcity would soon arise as a result of so many living so close together coupled with the need to prepare, for the forthcoming winter would force families to start leaving this large camp very soon. According to *Wawatum,* no more than about one hundred and fifty people could live together for any length of time if they were subsisting from the land in this region.

To my own dissatisfaction, one of the warriors whom I encountered in our camp was the unpleasant and sullen *Wenniway* who, despite the many presents he had received to relinquish his claim to me, continued to taunt and threaten me. He apparently believed that I had treated him unfairly while he was trying to cut my throat. Among the Indians, it is unknown to strike someone with their hands in anger, and this practice extends even to naughty children. They are therefore unfamiliar with the art of punching with a closed fist.

Wenniway apparently thinks that I used magic to escape his clutches when I succeeded in knocking him into momentary unconsciousness with my punch. Needless to say, *Wenniway* has a grudge, and I am anxious to avoid him.

Making my situation on Mackinac Island even more tenuous, a brigade of Montréal canoes bound for Michilimackinac was stopped by a swarm of small canoes from our camp as it passed between the island and Saint Ignace. The guide of the brigade admitted that their cargo was consigned to an English trader, and as a result, it was immediately plundered and produced, among other goods, some small kegs of rum. Drunkenness again broke out, and *Wawatum* feared he could not protect me.

As it was getting dark and the noise of a drunken frolic was intensifying, *Wawatum* decided to hide me away until the rum was consumed. He led me in the twilight up a steep path for a mile or more to a rocky cliff where there was a cave. The entrance, which I could barely make out in the gloom, was ten feet wide with the cave

CHARLES CLELAND

being quite shallow and rounded. It was fully dark, and *Wawatum* soon departed, telling me as he left to take shelter in the cave until he returned. I cut some small branches for a bed and assembled them inside and then entered the cave where, wrapping myself in my blanket, I soon fell fast asleep.

In the early dawn, I was awakened by a hard object under my blanket. I reached down to remove it and discovered it was a bone that I assumed was from a bear that had perhaps once used the cave as a den. I drifted back to sleep until awakened again by full bright sunlight. Looking around, I was horrified to discover that I was lying upon a heap of human bones and skulls that covered the entire floor of the cave. I hastily exited the place and sat waiting nearby the whole day for *Wawatum*, who did not appear. It occurred to me that *Wawatum* may have enjoyed some of the captured rum. I, on the other hand, was both thirsty and hungry; and as dark approached, I could not bear to spend another night in the charnel cave. I chose instead to spread my blankets under a bush. The morning dawned gray with a light drizzle and with me more than a little depressed.

In this state of despondency, I decided to review my decision to be a fur trader on the far wilderness frontier. After three years of "adventure," I had just awakened wet and hungry with a bush for a roof, and my only possession, the clothes on my back. I had been beaten senseless, nearly drowned on several occasions, starved to the verge of death, frozen, and nearly had my throat cut, let alone being the intended main course for a savage feast, and now I had been left to sleep with the dead. On the plus side, I had been moderately successful in selling goods and collecting furs; and while I had some credit with Montréal and Albany banks, my goods and furs had been plundered, and I was, at least for the present, without the resources to make a living. I had, however, learned the trade of a fur merchant and most of the skills of survival in the wilderness. In addition, I had learned the very complex language of the Ojibwe and Odawa Indians and had a passing knowledge of the French tongue.

So far, almost all things Indian were still mysterious to me. I had witnessed their absolute savagery in war as well as some customs which seemed utterly barbaric. Yet I also had experienced absolute kindness and generosity from Indians on several occasions, and in fact, I owed my life to their kindness. With my adoption by *Wawatum*, I felt for the first time the pleasures of being part of a complete family.

I thought back on the warning of my uncle and his insistence on the God-given divide between the savage and civilized races. Clearly my experience so far leaves that question open. I still do not know if the behavior of humans is driven by our inner nature or the rules that govern our societies. I don't exactly know why I want to better understand this puzzle, but it is one I need to resolve and so I can at least conclude that my adventure is not yet over. In the meantime, I await *Wawatum*.

CHARLES CLELAND

CHAPTER 10

I N THE LATE afternoon of my second day waiting at the burial cave, *Wawatum* finally appeared. I was very hungry, and even though I had found a seep from which I could suck up a bit of water, I was also extremely thirsty. We returned to our lodge, and *Wabigonkwe* had food and drink waiting for me.

Just as *Wawatum* had predicted, Mackinac Island, with all its solitude and beauty, could not support a large group of people who were getting their sustenance from the land. Our family, as well as others in the encampment, needed to leave the island to find food. As I knew personally, hunger is an occasional problem for hunters and gatherers because a steady supply of food is not always available, although hunger is always unrelenting. Indian people accept this as an inconvenient fact of life, but don't complain about hunger; they do, however, talk incessantly about food and where, when, and how to get it.

I learned that they have several successful strategies to maintain a steady supply of food. One of the most basic of these is moving from place to place as food sources become abundant in those places. In this way, they can take advantage of such temporary abundance as berry patches in season, schools of spawning fish, and flocks of migratory waterfowl. Another strategy is the seasonal round. Each year, native people such as my family undertake a journey from the shores and islands that are their homes during the warm season to the shelter of the deep woods of the interior during the winter. In each place, they were best situated to find the most possible food in those particular seasons.

Perhaps the most important means of assuring a steady supply of food is the custom of sharing. In Indian society, everyone is constantly giving things to each other, including tools, labor, and particularly food. Such exchanges are regulated by the etiquette embedded within kinship relationships. Since any one hunter may go many days between kills, the meat gifted by successful hunters is crucial in evening out the overall food supply among related families. As *Wawatum* put it, "We feed each other with meat and good will."

In leaving Mackinac Island, many families went to a large fishing village on the extreme western end of Bois Blanc Island, but *Wawatum* elected to take us to the more secluded waters of Saint Martin's Bay where we would fish for sturgeon. Before we made this trip, however, we had two other tasks to attend to, both at the insistence of *Wabigonkwe* and *Anangons*. The first was to make cord to replace laces on the cradleboard of *Anangons's* baby. These would be made from the fibers of stinging nettles, and since our fishing enterprise would also require strong line, *Wawatum* decided that we would go to the Les Cheneaux Islands where the family had already cached the necessary fibers earlier in the summer.

The second task, initiated by the women, was a complete makeover of my appearance so that I would look like an Ojibwe. This, they claimed, was motivated by their fear that I would be attacked if I were recognized as an Englishman. I knew I had little choice but to agree to their plan since if I have learned anything during my time with the Indians it was that Ojibwe women were tough and persistent. Once they set their minds to something you may as well do it.

Accordingly, *Wabigonkwe* and *Anangons* set to work. They first cut my hair and shaved my head, except for a spot above my ear on the side of my head about twice the size of the crown piece. This hair was braided, and it hung below my shoulder. I noted that they carefully removed all my white "skunk hair" since it is by this feature that I am recognized in this country. My face was painted with a broad green line across my forehead and a narrow red line under my eyes and across the bridge of my nose. A shirt was given to me that was painted with vermillion mixed with grease. A necklace of white wampum beads was hung around my neck, and silver bands decorated my upper arms and wrists. *Wabigonkwe* left us, and *Anangons* finished my makeover. Amid lots of giggling, she removed my trousers and covered each of my legs with a *midass,* a kind of hose made of scarlet cloth that was secured by a string tied to a belt. This same belt also supports a breech clout which is a strip of soft-tanned hide that passes between the legs and then over the belt in both the front and the back. I was then given a red blanket with a black stripe and a pair of beaded moccasins. Thus attired, *Anangons* flirted shamelessly with me, declaring that I was a

CHARLES CLELAND

very handsome Ojibwe man, at least much more handsome than the Englishman who was my former self. Strangely, I did not have the feeling that I was disguised as an Ojibwe. As far as I could see into the future, I would be hunting, fishing, and gathering furs that I would trade for the essentials. In short, I not only looked like an Indian; I was also rapidly becoming one.

It was mid-July when we pushed off our canoes for Saint Martin's Bay, and our route took us across Moran Bay, where in the previous century, the Jesuit priests had established a mission on the shore for refugee Huron Indians. From our position on the bay, *Wawatum* called my attention to a point of land which in profile looks like a reclining human figure. He explained that this was the final resting place of the mischievous spirit-person called *Nanabush*, who is also sometimes known as *Kitchiwaboose* or the "great hare." It is for this reason that the point is known as Rabbits Back Point. I hoped to learn more about *Nanabush*, but *Wawatum* told me that tradition forbid discussion of such matters until the month of *Gitchimanidogiizis*, or January. Then he told me that when the snow is deep in the woods and the nights are long around the fire, I would hear much of this important one.

We soon reached the Saint Martin's Islands and camped on the larger of the two. The next morning, we again got into our canoes and paddled east to a group of islands along the coast that were in the territory of *Wawatum's* relatives. Arriving at one of the larger islands, we drew out our canoes on a gravel beach near the southeast side. We carried our canoes to a small lake that was but a few yards from the shore of Lake Huron. This little lake was a hidden jewel, a smooth mirror reflecting all the trees and plants on its banks so perfectly that if it were not for the gentle ripples made by our gliding canoes, there would be nothing to distinguish nature's reality. It seemed to me that this lake, like the whole of the Ojibwe world, blurred the boundary between reality and illusion. In short order, we found the place along the shore where the family had sunk a pile of nettles that had now been in the water for several months. During this time, the green parts had rotted away, leaving only the tough stem fibers. These we collected and cleaned and then partially dried in the sun. By evening, our bounty was loaded, and we returned to Saint Martin's Bay.

The following day, the women separated and continued to dry the fibers; after that, they rolled them on their bare thighs to produce and connect the fiber strands to make cord so strong that I could not break it. Just as it was a woman's job to prepare the fibers and to make them into cords, it was the work of men to actually braid the cords into ropes and string. *Miigwan* helped me to learn the technique, but my ropes had weak spots and kinks. *Miigwan* told me we would save them in case I needed to climb a cliff.

The sturgeon is a large scaleless fish that is protected by bony plates; they are bottom feeders and prefer waters where shellfish and the larva of water insects are abundant. Really large sturgeon can reach eight feet in length and can weigh two hundred pounds, although most are smaller. As they are large and powerful enough to tear apart nets, the Ojibway preferred to take them with harpoons. *Wawatum* and *Miigwan* armed themselves with harpoons that were about thirty feet in length. At one end was a multibarbed bone point that was affixed into a socket on the shaft with pine pitch. A rope was tied to the point by means of a hole drilled for that purpose, and the line was passed up the shaft where it was held by the harpooner. A small white feather was also glued to the harpoon point to help the harpooner see it in very deep water.

Wawatum guided us to a spot on the leeside of Saint Martin's Island where there was a sandy basin in about twenty-five feet of water. The water was so clear that we could make out the ghostly shapes of many huge sturgeon lying on the bottom. At this point, *Miigwan* made the observation that he thought it was strange that there were so many sturgeon in the summer and so many bears around in the fall but that you never saw many sturgeon and bear at the same season. *Wawatum* explained that the reason this was so was because sturgeon and bear are really the same animal-person, which use different bodies at different times. He then produced tobacco which he spread on the water as a gift for the sturgeon spirit and offered a prayer. He prayed that the sturgeon would consent to give their bodies to us for food, and in exchange, we would not offend their spirits by taking more fish than we could use or allow dogs to gnaw their bones.

The harpoons were then slowly lowered into the water until the white feather was over a certain place above the sturgeon's body. *Wawatum* pointed out to me that the water spirits tried to protect their fish by bending the fisherman's harpoon so that it would miss the fish. Nonetheless, our harpoons were thrust, and the barbed points went into the great fish, and the poles became detached by their thrashing.

CHARLES CLELAND

The line attached to the point, which remained in the fish, went taut as the fish easily pulled our canoe through the water. As the sturgeon finally tired, we pulled them to our boat and, in this way, secured four fish, each weighing over a hundred pounds. We took these back to Saint Martin's Island where our family immediately began to cut them up into smaller pieces to smoke and dry on racks we built over low fires. This meat would help us get to our wintering grounds.

By early August, we were back on Mackinac Island and making serious preparation for our long trip to *Wawatum*'s family's hunting territory. During the next few weeks, all our energies were spent gathering, making, and repairing equipment such as canoes, traps, and snowshoes as well as packing dried food, clothing, medicine, cordage, glue, and other necessities. In the midst of this frenzy, I determined that I needed to return to Fort Michilimackinac in the hope of retrieving my Pennsylvania rifle, knife, and war ax that I had cached when, during the attack on the fort, it became apparent that my possessions would be plundered. I had wrapped these valuables in my panther cape and then in a sheet of oilcloth and hidden them under my house. *Wawatum* tried hard to dissuade me from returning but to no avail. Finally, seeing that I was going to go despite his best advice to the contrary, he asked *Miigwan* to go with me. We departed early the next morning and paddled across the straits to the fort. Although we saw my enemy *Wenniway* lounging outside the palisade, he did not recognize me in my Indian attire, and we succeeded in entering the fort without being noticed.

My house was unused, so I entered and discovered that the trap door to my storage cellar had been opened and emptied of its contents. I entered the small cellar and removed several of the upright pales which formed its walls; this permitted me to reach into the space between the ground surface and the house floor. To my delight, I felt my bundle undisturbed. *Miigwan* and I immediately returned to our canoe and paddled back to Mackinac Island.

By the end of August, we were ready for our journey. We had two canoes of twenty-two and twenty-five feet; one was paddled by *Miigwan* and *Anangons* who were accompanied by their baby and four dogs, plus some of the baggage. The larger canoe was paddled by *Wawatum, Wabigonkwe,* and me; our vessel contained most of the heavy baggage and the nightly camping gear. Our little company set out on a bright September day in the year 1762, with a slight warm breeze out of the south. Before crossing the Straits of Mackinac, *Wawatum* brought our brigade to a drift while he performed a time-honored ritual to appease the malevolent water spirit *Michipishiew*. This creature was thought to live under the water in the form of a panther with a huge, long tail which it thrashed to produce storms on the lakes. *Wawatum* sacrificed a white dog, which was thrown into the lake with his feet tied while he asked *Michipishiew* for safe passage down the coast of *Michigami*, the big lake.

We camped the first night among the Odawa at L'Arbre Croche where I encountered *Ogamachumaki*, one of the Odawa chiefs who had saved me from a fateful trip to Beaver Island earlier in the summer. We passed a pleasant evening with him, and he gave me a token of good fortune which was a small polished fossil stone with curious pentagonal markings; each of which had a black center so to resemble eyes. *Ogamachumaki* told me the stones were only found in the country of the Odawa. I carry it still.

We left L'Arbre Croche at first light and headed south amid small rolling waves. All along, the coast we saw an almost continuous vista of Odawa homesteads and fields. In a place where a narrow peninsula creates a small harbor beneath a great headland, we struck south across a broad bay called Petite Traverse by the voyagers. We reached the opposite shore at a place the Odawa call *Bashoo,* which means "nearby" in reference to their village at the head of the bay.

Further along, we came to a place on the shore where the clear waters revealed huge boulders littering the lake bed and shore. This place was called *Kitchiossining* or big rock known as a prime fishing spot for lake trout. Yet farther on, we came to a small shallow stream running with great strength into *Michigami* between high sandbanks. So beautiful, we decided to explore it; *Wawatum* said it was called *Zhiingwaakziibii* or Pine River. Although the high bluffs along the lake with their giant white pines were magnificent, this sight was nothing compared to the vista which awaited us a short way up the winding stream. Here, we beheld a magical small round lake whose blues waters reflected the orange, red, and yellow foliage of the surrounding forest. This lake in turn received an outlet of water from a very large lake that we could see winking through the trees at its far end. It was truly a wondrous place, and we left it reluctantly.

About ten miles south of Pine River is the most famous spot among the Indians on the entire *Michigami* coast. It is marked by a

CHARLES CLELAND

twelve-foot-high cliff of white stone on the shore that provides veins of chert, a flintlike rock that ancient tribesmen depended upon to chip into useful tools and weapons. It is known far and wide as *Pewangoing,* or "place of the flint." The Ojibwe believed that the chert was formed from the bones of one of their original spirit ancestors. We camped that night on the small sandy beach about one mile south of the chert quarry, a place where we could see our next objective. This is a point of land on the horizon about ten miles distant which we had to reach by crossing the mouth of a very large bay exposed to the open water of the big lake. The Canadian voyagers called this crossing place the Grand Traverse.

The next morning, a brisk west wind kicked up waves that *Wawatum* judged to be dangerous for our heavily laden canoes. So we had a day to rest. We hunters climbed a steep bluff behind the beach, and I was fortunate to be able to kill a large doe whose meat provided a welcome change in diet from dried sturgeon and corn. I killed the deer with a long shot, and I was pleased to find my long rifle working in good order. As is their Ojibwe custom, *Wawatum* and *Miigwan* gave me high praise as a good shot and a skillful hunter. I, in turn, gave each of them the portion of the deer which custom required; thus, my father received a haunch and my brother the heart and liver. I would later give *Wabigonkwe* the mother's portion and the choice back strap to *Anangons.* This latter was the wife's portion which I gave to *Anangons* as my sister-in-law.

The wind dropped the next morning, and we set out again, successfully crossing the Grand Traverse and rounding the point on the other side. After a brief rest, we again headed south passing a good-sized stream that drained a large inland lake. We camped in view of two islands on the western horizon both backlit at sunset by a solid gray sky that came close to the horizon, leaving a narrow band between the water and sky when the sun set; this strip became blood red as the sun went down. These islands are called the *Manitous,* or the "spirit islands," but for what reason *Wawatum* did not know. The next day, we paddled past mountains of yellow sand which plunged steeply into the lake on the shore to our east. These dunes are an unmistakable landmark for travelers, and *Wabigonkwe*, in her practical yet mischievous way, said, "Some people say that these dunes look like crouching bears, but I think they just look like big sand dunes."

Futher to the south we passed the mouth of a very large river which deposits a plume of dark water as it enters the big lake. Here we observed the smoke from many cooking fires coming from a large Indian village. Late in the day, we found a small sandy stream that flows through a cluster of dunes from a large marshy embayment behind them. This was Sand River known to the voyagers as the Aux Sable. It is this river which is the doorway to *Wawatum's* hunting ground. He had been here many times as a child with his father and grandfather and knew the country with certainty. The estuary of the river was filled with migrating waterfowl, and as our canoes glided across a small lake, we saw many signs of beaver. As a result, *Wawatum* suggested that we spend a month at this location and directed us to a traditional camping spot.

Our semipermanent camp was located on a small peninsula directly across the lake from the outflow of the Aux Sable River. This site gave us ready access to a large bayou, not to mention the abundant marshland bordering the lake. During the next month, we spent our time here hunting, primarily the beaver but also raccoons, mink, and otters. The skins of the beaver are the currency of the country so that the worth of any object of trade, including the skins of other animals, can be calculated at its value in beaver pelts. The trade in beaver, as I well know from my former occupation, is an international enterprise there being an insatiable demand for this item in Europe. There, the beaver pelt is processed to remove the course guard hairs, leaving the soft under fur. The remaining fur is then ground up to be used in the manufacture of felt. The felt is, in turn, manufactured into hats, mostly of the three-corner variety that are now very popular in Europe and in the American colonies.

In hunting the beaver, we used several methods in the autumn season, which include shooting them as they swim in the open water and taking them in steel traps or snares that we set along their travel routes. We avail ourselves very much of this prior method each evening when the animals become active and go abroad to fix their dams and houses and to seek food. We paddle up the stream and then drift down with the current; the beaver pay us no mind so we can drift close enough to kill them with a musket shot. Since my rifle is much more accurate than the muskets that the Indians acquire from the traders, I soon acquired the reputation of a good provider. During the winter, we set traps under the ice or, if possible, break up the beaver lodges where

CHARLES CLELAND

whole families of beaver could be found. Much of our diet in the fall is made up of the flesh of this animal; the tail we especially relish.

Much of the work of the fur trade falls to the women who skin the animals, stretch the hides on wooden frames, and then scrape away the fat and flesh from the underside of the skins so that they do not spoil and drop the fur. Once prepared, the skins are packed into heavy bales for transport.

I confess that I am much enjoying the life of a hunter. To be sure, our whole family works constantly from sunup until well past dark each day. Since I was raised to the same long hours of work, the routine is familiar to me. Unlike my earlier farm labor, our work now is often a communal affair full of good-natured banter and joking. This work tradition provides a division of labor that assigns specific tasks to each person according to their age and gender. In this way, the vital work of daily life is accomplished by a family partnership where each person can feel the importance of their contributions, be these knowledge, skill, or labor.

CHAPTER 11

L OW GRAY CLOUDS began to dominate our skies, and as the temperature crept steadily lower, *Wawatum* became more and more anxious to move the family further up the river. He feared that we would get trapped near the coast by a sudden deep, cold snap that would freeze the Au Sable, making our canoes useless and forcing us to carry all our gear on our backs for many miles. This situation occasioned my first disagreement with *Wawatum*. Since we were catching many beaver each day, I contended that we should take the risk and stay where we were in order to continue to reap the rich harvest of furs a while longer. I told him we could earn a great many credits with the traders, and in this way, we could get many more goods. *Wawatum* told me that what I was saying was true but that we already had all the goods we needed.

"Why do we need three axes each, and how many guns could we possibly carry?" Not satisfied with this quite conclusive argument, he asked two more questions of me.

"If we don't hunt, what do you think we will eat when winter comes? And can you carry a one-hundred-pound pack on a five-day march?"

He concluded his argument by saying that I was free to stay or go as I wished but that he and the others would be heading up the river just as his family had done for generations. Although his arguments did not seem economically rational to me, I knew they made practical sense in every way. I would go up the river.

On one of our last days on the embayment, *Miigwan* and I had gone upriver in the afternoon and were returning with two large and one small beaver and a raccoon. As we approached our camp, we saw a strange canoe pulled up at our landing site. A man, who I did not know, was stepping out of our lodge, causing me to immediately put down my paddle and pick up my rifle.

Miigwan quickly put his hand on my arm as he recognized the man as *Anangons*'s father. We landed, and *Miigwan* greeted his father-in-law with respectful enthusiasm and introduced me. Our voices brought everyone else spilling out from the lodge laughing and talking, and I was introduced to *Anangons*'s mother and younger sister. Her sister's name was *Zenibaakwe* or "Ribbon Woman." She was very lively, in constant motion with an active, happy face and sparkling black eyes, and I guessed she was about seventeen years old. *Anangons*'s mother was from all appearances a *metis*. She was tall and slender like *Anangons* with very light skin. She wore a full cloth skirt in the fashion of the French and spoke the Odawa dialect with a slight French accent but, in all other ways, dressed and acted like an Odawa woman. Her name was Jolie.

I learned that our visitors were from a village on the mouth of the Manistee River that was not far to our north and that they had come expressly to find us before we disappeared into the interior forests. *Anangons* was very excited to see her parents and sister and to hear all the news of her family and friends.

It was during their visit that I made a startling discovery about the broader implications of my new kinship position within the Ojibwe family. I was busily working around the camp the next morning carving a new canoe paddle when I overheard *Anangons* and *Zenibaakwe* laughing and speculating rather loudly about the size of my *niinag* or "penis." Seeing that I had heard them, they asked me, "Is it as long as your middle finger?" I can only say that I was mortified by their crude remarks and stomped off, my face burning bright red with embarrassment, which only occasion more laughter.

That afternoon when *Miigwan* and I were alone checking beaver traps, I decided to question him about the behavior of his wife and sister-in-law. This is where I received a great revelation. I repeated the incident and was surprised when I got a good chuckle from *Miigwan*. Still smiling, *Miigwan* said, "As you are familiar kin to *Anangons*, that is, an in-law of the opposite sex, good fun is always to be expected between you. This custom," he said, "comes from the fact that, by tradition, if I were to die, you would likely become *Anangons*'s husband, and our baby would become your child."

Miigwan continued with a mischievous smile on his face, "Another thing which might happen is that I may take *Zenbaakwe* as a second wife. In fact, *Anangons* is begging me to do just that. She says she needs help with her work. If I had two wives and died, you might inherit them both. So," he concluded, "that is why *Anangons* and *Zenbaakwe* are curious about your *niinag.*"

All I could manage for a reply was "Oh my god!"

Seeing my shock and consternation, *Miigwan* almost fell out of the canoe with uncontrollable laughter. When he recovered, he explained the more serious side of these customs. "You may have noticed that there are practically no widows or orphans among the Ojibwe or, for that matter, very few single adults. This is because marriage is not only a bond between individuals but between families and bands. These in-law bonds created by marriage are important to our economy and social life and therefore to our survival. Kin provides the avenues to shared food and access to the resources of the territories of other bands in time of need. In fact, the in-law bonds created by marriage are so vital that our customs keep them alive even if one of the partners in a marriage dies."

Even though I had not the least intention of obtaining a wife, I began to take a more serious interest in *Anangons*'s welfare, and even, on occasion, I ventured a risqué joke at her expense which always elicited a big smile.

Besides a family visit, *Anangons*'s parents had come to our camp because her father had been invited by *Anangons* and *Miigwan* to name their baby. *Anangons*'s father, *Manitou Maaiingun,* or "Spirit Wolf" was frequently chosen by members of his band as a name giver because his names brought good fortune to their recipients. Accordingly, *Anangons* organized a naming ceremony that started with *Manitou Maaiingun* relating his name dream for the baby. In his dream, it was a time of famine when the people were suffering cruelly from hunger. He saw a large pond, and there was a girl who was running around the pond. As she made her fourth circuit around the shore, the surface of the water began to dimple and splash, as if it were raining, yet the sky was perfectly clear. Looking more closely, he saw that the water was being disturbed by swarms of grasshoppers which were jumping into the water to escape the running girl. This drew many fish to the surface to eat the insects. The girl quickly grabbed a scoop net and caught a great pile of fish, which she gave to the people to save them from starvation.

Manitou Maaiingun said that the baby would be named *Papakinkwe* or "Grasshopper Woman" and that she would be a good food finder for her people. *Manitou Maaiingun* then picked up the child and held her tight against his chest so that she would absorb the power of his dream.

With little *Papakin*, as we called her for short, introduced to her family, *Anangons* gave presents to all in attendance and served a feast of fish, beaver, wild rice, and corn soup. *Wawatum* blessed the feast and our gathering, sending his prayers aloft with the smoke of his pipe.

As the first large snowflakes laced with heavy pellets of sleet descended from the dark gray overcast, we said our good-byes to *Anangons*'s family and headed up river. When after a few days of paddling the river narrowed, and we reached the limits of canoe travel, we camped and built a winter rack for our canoes and a tree cache for our furs and some emergency food. *Wawatum* and *Miigwan* cleverly built the cache so that it would be out of the reach of wolves and other hungry marauders. We also made up packs of all the items we would need to survive a winter in the deep forest. The packs of the women, which would be carried with the aid of trump lines, were by far the heaviest, well, over one hundred pounds. Those of the men, who would be hunting and protecting the family along the trail, weighed much less. My pack weighed least of all because as *Wawatum* observed in jest, but truthfully, "Englishmen can only carry half as much as an Ojibwe woman."

Before setting out, however, we celebrated the annual Feast of the Dead in honor of our departed ancestors and friends. We were not permitted to enter our lodge until well after dark, and then I was told to sit in complete silence as "the dead do not like noise." We sat for what seemed like a long time, and then *Wawatum* began a long oration in which he evoked the spirits of our ancestors and friends by calling out the names of the deceased and asking them and others dear to us to be present. He asked them to assist us in our forthcoming hunt and to eat the food prepared for them. I must say that in the quiet, dark lodge, I did feel the presence of my parents, poor John Jamet and Mr. Tracy; and then, unaccountably, I suddenly knew with certainty that my friend, the giant Scot warrior, Angus Campbell, had lost his life on some distant battlefield and that his spirit was among us too.

Wawatum handed each of us two ears of partially boiled corn which was slow eating. He asked that we not break the cobs as that would displease the departed. When we finished, *Wawatum* kindled a new fire from a fresh spark. A pipe was smoked, and the dozen cobs were neatly buried in a hole dug inside the lodge. This done *Wawatum* began to sing and to beat a drum, and the whole family had a pleasant time dancing around the fire for the greater part of the night. This feast took place on the first day of November.

Then, on the first day of the "Moon of the Little Spirits," we shouldered our packs and began the march to our hunting camp, covering almost twenty miles that day. This regime was repeated for two more days, so I calculated that we were about fifty or sixty miles inland from the coast of *Michigami*. We finally arrived at the site where the family typically camped for the winter in a sheltered valley with a small stream. While *Wabigonkwe, Anangons,* and *Miigwan* were setting up lodges, *Wawatum* and I decided to hunt in hopes of finding fresh meat for dinner. I went in one direction while he went in the other.

I immediately came across a fresh deer trail and began to track the animal which was difficult because of the fact that the snow was thin and patchy. Consequently, I had to keep circling outward and back in order to cut the animal's trail. In my enthusiasm, I lost my sense of direction, and it quickly became dark. After realizing I had no idea how to find my way back, I gave up and started a fire with my rifle flint and wrapped myself in my blanket and went to sleep in the shelter of a huge downed tree trunk.

When I awoke in the morning, the sky was heavily overcast, so I had no way to determine direction. I fired my rifle twice and hoped to hear a return shot, but I heard only the wind in the empty trees. Initially, I was not too distressed to be alone in the woods since I could provide for myself with my rifle, and I had no fear of the wilderness. I also was well aware, however, that I was alone in a forest which stretched unbroken for hundreds of miles in all directions. I also knew well that the winter forest was filled with mortal perils for lone individuals. As I inventoried the possible dangers in my mind, an intense fear suddenly loomed before me and in fact overtook me. My heart started to pound, and I began to walk rapidly and sometimes to run blindly toward no place in particular.

I spent another lonely night, an incredibly miserable one on account of a cold rain that turned to heavy snow by dawn. I had built a lean-to the previous evening and huddled in it now, wet, cold, and hungry with no idea of where to go. I fired my gun again but heard no reply. On one of my short forays to collect dry wood for my sputtering fire, I saw the frozen surface of a lake through the trees. Further inspection proved it was a very large lake since I could hardly make out the opposite shore.

I had not heard *Wawatum* or *Miigwan* speak about a lake of this size in their territory, so I decided not to venture in that direction.

As I thought more about my situation, plans for rational action gradually replaced blind panic. I decided I could best find my family by going west, back toward *Michigami*. The sun was still hidden in the clouds, however, but the snow had stopped. I thought about one of *Wawatum*'s lessons regarding directions. He had said that limbs are more numerous and larger on the south side of trees and that moss grows more abundantly on the north side of the tree trunks and that streams along the coast generally fall from the east to the west. Following these clues, I began to travel in the direction that I hoped was west. Since it was early December, the days were very short; in fact, it was dark by late afternoon; and the snow, although not deep enough to absolutely require snowshoes, was difficult to walk through. Walking in deep snow and in cold weather requires much energy, and since I had no food, I could not replace what I burned. I prepared to spend my third night lost in the woods.

I gathered some tinder for my evening fire and went to my rifle to get the flint. To my horror, I discovered that the gun flint has slipped from the jaws of my gun cock and was lost. The enormity of this discovery struck wild fear into my heart. I had no way to start a fire, get food, or protect myself, all of which depended upon that one little piece of stone. My panic experienced earlier in the day was now replaced by a feeling of total helplessness.

I constructed another crude shelter of cedar limbs, rolled myself up in my blanket, and tried to sleep. The howling of wolves not far distant from my miserable camp did not provide a restful environment for slumber. I did finally sleep and woke before dawn, hungry and cold. As the day broke, it became apparent that the sky was clearing, and I could see a red sunrise to the east. To my immense relief, I had indeed been traveling west the previous day. I set out on the same course and, in the late morning, came to a small lake with a beaver lodge along the bank. I walked toward the lodge thinking I could perhaps break it down and somehow catch a beaver for food. As I approached the lodge, I saw that it had already been broken into. As I studied this place, I suddenly realized that during the previous fall, *Miigwan* and I had been the ones who destroyed the lodge.

This discovery gave me a better idea of where I might find my family's camp, so I adjusted my course to the north and east and marched on for the rest of the day. I knew that I was getting very weak, and I camped again without heat or food, and I was afraid to sleep for fear I would freeze to death in the night.

The next morning, I knew I could not last much longer, and I set out, generally following a small brook. As I was walking down a long hill at midday, I saw a large trail in the snow in the valley below. From a distance, I took it for elk tracks; but when I came closer, I discovered it was a relatively fresh snowshoe track, perhaps a day old. I cannot describe the relief and joy I felt at that moment. I followed the track for several hours, but I could only move very slowly. Just as the sun was beginning to sink in the western sky, I smelled the faint aroma of wood smoke; and soon after, I heard the distant barking of a dog.

I walked on but was about done in. Finally, I yelled out *aanii*, "hello," since I didn't exactly know if this was our camp or that of some other Indian family. To my great joy, I heard *Wabigonkwe* calling, "*Zhigaag! Zhigaag!*" As I made my way the last one hundred yards, the family came spilling out of the lodge and, along with our pack of dogs, rushed to me. They were all talking at once, and tears were streaming down all our faces. They had all but given me up for dead, convinced that I had fallen victim to *Windigo*, the cannibal giant of the north woods. I was never so glad to be home.

CHARLES CLELAND

CHAPTER 12

THE NEVER-CEASING WEST wind blowing over the open water of *Michigami* brought snow nearly every day until by January, we were literally buried. A deep freeze accompanied the snow, stilling our small stream, so we were obliged to melt snow to get water. On most days, the energy required to hunt was not worth the poor return, since the deer and elk were not moving far from the thick shelter of the cedar swamps. Snowshoe hare, taken with snares, were about our only fresh meat; and though tasty, rabbit flesh is very lean and does not provide much energy. The family spent most days lounging around our *wigwam*.

Our winter wigwam is built on a frame of aspen poles bent and tied together to form a dome which is about twelve feet in width and fifteen feet long. The form is covered with mats woven from cattails as well as large sheets of birch bark tied in such a way as to overlap and shed rain and snow. A hole is left at the apex for smoke to escape but, on many occasions, did not work very well so that our eyes become red and itchy from the irritation of the smoke. An opening is also left on one side to provide a door that is covered with a blanket. This dwelling, although crowded with five adults and the baby, is easily heated by a small fire which burns in the center of the lodge.

Space in the wigwam is rigidly apportioned by Ojibwe custom. The male head of the household, in this case *Wawatum*, occupies the area immediately to the right of the doorway. The wife, *Wabigonkwe*, occupies the area to the left of the door. *Miigwan*, as the oldest son, has a space next to his father, while *Anangons* and baby *Papakine* are situated next to *Wabigonkwe* on the left side. I occupy a space at the center rear of the lodge directly opposite the doorway.

The paraphernalia of each person is located in their space so that guns, ammunition, spears, traps, drums, pipes, and other tools and implements used by *Wawatum* and *Miigwan* and me are located on the right side. The women's side is piled with bark boxes, or *makakoon,* which contain dishes, clothes, dried food, and implements for food preparation, sewing, and hide working. The high-domed ceiling is hung with ceremonial items such as medicine bags and regalia as well as large quantities of dried herbs used for spice and medicine. The back and side walls have a low platform for sleeping by night and lounging during the day. The floor is otherwise covered with woven mats. The dwelling is kept neat, clean, and sweet smelling by *Wabignokwe* who, like all Ojibwe housewives, reigns supreme inside the *wigwam.*

Besides our *wigwam,* our camp also consists of several exterior structures, including a food storage rack near the door that is secured from our dogs, a sweat lodge which looks like a small round version of our dwelling, and a menstrual hut that is cone shaped and covered by mats and bark. The latter structure becomes the temporary abode of *Anangons* during four days each moon when she is menstruating. During that time, she is waited upon by *Wabigonkwe* to assure that we men are not exposed to menstrual blood which is regarded as having maleficent power and would surely spoil our hunting success. There is a well-tramped path through the snow connecting these structures which is lined with piles of firewood. During the winter months, we spend much time together in our *wigwam.* There is not much conversation, except for the arrangement of chores, discussion of the weather, and possible locations of game animals, but we are amused by playing with little *Papakine* who, though generally swaddled in her cradleboard, is a happy, smiling child who carefully watches every activity around her. We are otherwise kept busy mending and making implements and clothing, especially warm footwear. I do, however, often find myself caught in deep boredom, although this malady does not affect the rest of the family who seems to have infinite patience. One diversion that does hold a deep interest for me is *Wawatum*'s storytelling, which contains elements of Ojibwe history, cosmology, and mythology. I must admit that my interest have been piqued by certain events that I had experienced after coming among the Ojibwe that I cannot explain by the rationale of my upbringing. Under *Wawatum*'s tutelage, I have soon come to understand that the spirit world of the Ojibwe is huge and complex and that by any measure, the Ojibwe are very religious people.

In the first instance, the Ojibwe believe the world was created by an all-powerful deity called *Kitchi Manitou* or "the Great Spirit" who is also sometimes referred to as the "the Great Mystery" or "the Master of Life." In any case, *Kitchi Manitou* laid down the founding elements of the world but does not seem to interfere in its day-to-day operation. That is left to the devices of hundreds of spirits, each of which has domain over a specific realm or location of the natural world. It is to the spirits that the Ojibwe appeal by prayer and sacrifice to try to affect outcomes in everyday matters.

As I could understand it, the foundation of Ojibwe spiritual life is based upon the belief that almost all things are possessed of a body, a soul or spirit, and a shadow. *Wawatum* explained that the body is the visible and material element of a being that is associated with the breath. The spirit is located in the heart and is the source of the being's intelligence. The shadow, which is not the shadow cast by the sun, is invisible but on occasion may be seen. For example, when we think we see someone in a crowd who we know is really very far away, it is because that person's shadow lets itself become visible for an instant. In essence, spirits and shadows are alike, except that they are gifted with different forces and powers. A spirit may also become separated from its body as when a person dreams or has a vision or is very drunk. This is a very powerful and dangerous state since there is the risk that the body and spirit may not be reunited, and then the possibility of insanity or even death may result. Some shamans, those who have the power to interact with the spirit world, also are thought to have the ability to willfully assume the bodies of animals or people. In a similar way, the same spirit may assume different body forms. Here, *Wawatum* reminded me that he once told us that sturgeons and bears were the same animal with different bodies.

Wawatum also pointed out that the world around us is made up of the sky dome, the sky, the earth's surface, and the underground world which are all full of spirits. Some roam around from place to place, while others stay in particular places. The world is dangerous because while some spirits are beneficial to humans, others harm humans, if they are not constantly placated. The only way humans can assure their welfare is to gain the power necessary to manipulate the spirits. Power is acquired through dreams or visions that provide spiritual helpers, charms, magical spells, and songs that influence the action of the spirits. *Wawatum* told me that this is why he sacrificed the dogs and tobacco to the underwater panther, Michipishiew to protect us on our long lake voyage. That spirit is known to like the flesh of dogs as well as tobacco. The fact that we traveled in good weather shows that *Wawatum*'s magic is strong.

Wawatum said that hunting is another good example of the necessity of keeping good relations with the spirits of game animals. He admitted that I was a good hunter and went on to speculate that I probably believed that this was because I was lucky and was a good shot with my long rifle. He said, however, that this was not the case. "Game," he said, "was killed not by the skill of hunter but because the animal we hunt can recognize the hunter's shadow and decides if it is willing to give up its body to the hunter. If it so desires, then that deer could be killed with any gun or bow or by any hunter. If, however, the dead deer's spirit is not pleased with the hunter's treatment of its body, or if the hunter is wasteful with the meat or greedy with its distribution, then this will be communicated to the spirits of living deer, and the hunter will not have further success."

"You see," *Wawatum* said, "you are a good hunter because you are a good man who is generous and in harmony with the spirits of the natural world. I, who also have some success in hunting, was blessed with a powerful hunting charm, which contains the power of the wolf. The wolf, as you know, is the most successful deer hunter of all. I call this charm, which I received during my youthful vision quest, *waawaashkeshii mashkiki* or 'deer medicine,' but that is not its true name. That name I cannot speak without diminishing the power of the charm." *Wawatum* then instructed me to always carry a quantity of tobacco which must be put down in offering to the spirit of any plant or animal that I might take for our own use.

The basic organization of the mythological world is embodied in the many stories which are well-known among the Ojibwe and serve as entertainment around the lodge fire. *Nanabush*, one of the original figures of the Ojibwe primeval dream time, wandered the newly formed earth where his encounters with people, animals, and supernatural creatures result in outrageous adventures of which many are risqué and often contrary to Ojibwe ethics and mores. In their telling, *Wawatum*, master storyteller that he is, often brings us to tears of mirth and gasps of disbelief. As one of *Nanabush*'s story leads to another, *Nanabush* is gradually transformed by experience from a bumbling fool who understands neither the function of his own body nor the proper social

CHARLES CLELAND

behavior of the Ojibwe to a collected and powerful guide to good behavior. Along the way, *Nanabush* intervenes in the natural order to create many features of the modern world—from the origin of corn to the robin's red breast—and hundreds of other familiar aspects of the world around us.

Whether it is their well-developed origin mythology or some other cause, the Ojibwe seem to have little curiosity about the order of the natural world which is so well explained in their oral tradition. I seldom hear discussions about why things are as they are, but on the other hand, there is great curiosity and apprehension about any unusual feature or occurrence. For example, a fox that sits near a trail and watches us passed without fear or even a small anatomical anomaly noticed while butchering an animal elicits great concern and discussion. This is because any deviation from the natural order is thought to be due to human agency and therefore raises a suspicion of witchcraft.

I might also observe that the Ojibwe are a people of unquestioning patience. Whereas I find myself wishing for warmer weather and fresh fruit and thinking about such pleasures as regular bathing, my family seems perfectly content with whatever conditions are at hand. I have never heard them complain with their lot, whether it is hunger, mosquitoes, cold, or sickness.

Sometime during the "sucker moon" or February, and I confess that I had lost all track of the date or day of the week, I grew bored with being snowbound in the *wigwam* and decided to make a short deer hunt hoping to at least break the monotony of dried food. At some little distance from our dwelling, I noticed a huge oak tree that had been damaged in a storm to such an extent that a great limb had splintered off the trunk, which appeared to be hollow. I noticed that the small limbs above the opening were covered with a thick layer of frost and that the trunk near the ground had many deep scratches. My examination of the tree led me to conclude that a bear was hibernating in the hollow trunk, and the frost was from his condensed breath.

When I returned home, I reported my find, and the possibility of killing a bear much excited the entire family. Beside the prospect of fresh meat, our diet of lean dried meat gave us a strong craving for fat, and we knew that a hibernating bear would have much of that commodity. Fat could also be rendered to produce oil for which there are many uses. Another large warm sleeping robe would also be welcomed. To get to the bear, if one was indeed present, would require us to cut down the tree with our light camp axes as we did not have a heavy felling ax. After discussion, we decided to make the effort; and the next day, the whole family commenced chopping. After laboring all day, without successfully bringing the tree down, we were forced to continue our efforts the next morning. By noon, the old giant was swaying back and forth, and *Wawatum* suggested that the women continue to chop while the men take up more distance positions with their guns and prepare to shoot the bear, if one emerged.

I judged where the top of the tree would probably fall and stationed myself a good fifty yards from that spot so that I would have a clear field of fire. *Wawatum* and *Miigwan* positioned themselves on each side and close to the trunk. The women chopped on, and we soon heard a loud cracking sound as the tree began to fall in my direction. It came slowly at first, but its enormous weight caused it to gain speed, and its force smashed all the other trees in its path. It hit the ground so hard that it literally shook the forest floor. Clouds of snow and broken limbs rained down, momentarily obscuring my vision. In that instant, a great bear appeared in the haze before me; it rose on its hind legs and looked directly at me and then quickly dropped on all fours and came at me with tremendous speed. In that instant, I recognized the animal as the same one that was in my dream many years ago.

I threw up my long rifle and, in one brief moment, aimed and squeezed the trigger. The pan flashed, and a split second later, my gun discharged, sending a heavy ball which struck the bear's skull, killing it instantly. I sunk down in the snow trembling, the dead bear only a few dozen feet away. My first rational thought was that this bear's spirit did not seem to be entirely ready to give me its body.

Once we were sure the huge animal was dead, the family approached to examine it. My old mother, *Wabigonkwe*, began to wail; and she grasped the bear's head, fondling and kissing it; and then addressing the bear as *ninokoomis or* "grandmother," she began to beg the grandmother's forgiveness for having taken her life. In a tearful voice, she cried out, "Please have mercy on my family and please remember it was not us Ojibwe that killed you but the Englishman." I was the only one to appreciate the irony. All these lamentations and pleas for mercy did not deter us from gutting, skinning, and butchering our "grandmother" for our obligation to completely use all parts of the bear is part of our respectful conduct. The bear had six inches of fat on some parts of her body, and it took two of us just to carry the fat back to our *wigwam*. After butchering, we made up four packs of meat to return to our food cache. Together, I estimated that this huge female bear weighed at least five hundred pounds. *Wawatum* said she was the largest bear he had ever seen.

As soon as we reached our lodge, the bear's head was placed upon a scaffold where it was decorated with silver jewelry, wampum, red ribbon, and other decorative trinkets. A large quantity of tobacco was placed near its nose, since it is said that bears like tobacco as much as humans. The next morning as preparations were made for a feast honoring the spirit of the bear, I was reminded that bears were known to be a very powerful creature by the Ojibwe, all the more because they resembled humans in many ways. The *wigwam* was then cleaned and swept, and a new blanket was placed under the bear's head. Pipes were then lit, and *Wawatum* blew smoke into the nostrils of the bear. I was instructed to follow his example so that the bear's spirit would not be angry with me. At that point, I tried to persuade *Wawatum* that the bear was dead and that I had no fear of retribution from a dead bear. *Wawatum* replied that my attitude was both naïve and very dangerous. The food, being ready for feasting, *Wawatum* made an oration addressed to the spirit of the bear. The tenor of his remarks were that we deplored the necessity under which men must destroy their "friends," but this misfortune was unavoidable since, without doing so, men have no means to subsist. With the condolence ceremony concluded, we gorged on the fat and flesh of the bear, and after several days, we added her head to our kettle.

Although I do not consider myself to be a deep thinker, in retrospect, I had to appreciate *Wawatum*'s logic in considering the basic differences between humans and nonhuman persons, especially in the case of bears. After all, and irrespective of necessity, it is the humans through their own agency, who willfully interrupt the natural order, when they destroy nonhuman species. To do this, humans use the ability to employ spiritual power in order to manipulate the spirit world. Since this is the only path to their success as hunters and gatherers, they must maintain harmony with the spirit world and thereby their continuing ability to manipulate it. Factual support of this premise is found in what is certainly a self-fulfilling prophecy, namely that successful hunters continually confirm their ability to please the animal spirits while unsuccessful hunters demonstrate that they lack that same power. This it seems is not too different from the prayers of Christians, who also appeal to a supernatural force to intercede on their behalf by changing the flow of natural events. Beyond these philosophical musings, I also had a personal need to make peace with the bear, not because I had killed her but because I honestly believed that my relationship with this particular bear was rooted in the supernatural realm. I have no proof of this except that the moment the bear came out of the tree and looked at me, I knew absolutely it was true. I also admit to a deep sense of relief knowing that this bear, the bear of my dream, is indeed dead. However, if the Ojibwe view is correct, that bear's spirit, a bad spirit at that, is still roaming this world.

CHAPTER 13

WINTER SLOWLY RELEASED its grip during the month of March as the temperature bounced back and forth between above freezing during the day and below freezing at night. This fluctuation had two important benefits for hunters and gatherers such as us. The first was that it caused the sweet sap of the maple trees to rise, and the second was to form a crust on the deep snow. The Ojibwe call March *Onaabanigiizs* or the "crusty snow month." The benefit of crusty snow is that the hunter, with his snowshoes and dogs, can easily walk across the surface, but deer will break through the crust and must struggle to run as the sharp edges cut their legs. For this reason, we hunters were very successful; the three of us killed fifty-three deer by the middle of the month. This effort represents nearly four thousand pounds of meat most of which, when dried, will be taken to Michilimackinac for the trade.

One immediate problem was to get all our dried meat, fur and hides, and other camp gear back to the cache where we left our canoes in the autumn. This facility was about seventy miles from our hunting camp. I calculated that the five of us would have to carry nearly six tons this distance on our backs. To do this, we made up our packs and started moving early one morning. We carried until the midafternoon and then constructed a scaffold and cached our loads. We then returned to our *wigwam* and, the next morning, repeated the process as we did for several days afterward until we finally moved the camp itself. This entire process was repeated many times over the next three weeks of very hard labor until we finally got all our material to the canoes and our fur cache. By the time we reached the end of our carry, I was able to tote almost as much as *Wabigonkwe* and *Anangons*. Carrying was generally the work of women but was balanced on the trail against the responsibilities of the men whose hands and attention needed to be free to protect the family from dangers from either man or beast.

It now being April, which the Ojibwe call *ishkigamiziggeiizis* or the "maple sugar moon," we were about to reap the second benefit of the spring weather. We loaded our canoes and proceeded downstream headed for the maple sugaring grove where *Wawatum's* family traditionally gathered each spring. This place was located on the lower Au Sable River near *Michigami*. As we beached our canoes among those already drawn up at the sugar camp landing, we were engulfed by relatives who greeted us warmly. Although I had not met most of these people and was a foreigner, they nonetheless greeted me with enthusiasm and in no way different from *Miigwan*. In their eyes, we were both *Wawatum's* sons. I might also mention that *Anangon's* sister, *Zenbaakwe*, was also now living in this camp. Since we had seen her she had married one of *Miigwan's* cousins. Her behavior toward me was polite, friendly, but demure quite different from the flirtatious girl I had met the previous fall. Now she was a married woman, the wife of one of my kinsmen.

The main business of the camp, besides socializing, was the production of maple sugar, which was not only a food but also a market commodity. The camp had a very festive air, free of the long isolation of the winter hunting camps. Everyone was happy to see relatives and to hear the news. One of the main topics of conversation and the source of anxiety was the events at Fort Michilimackinac the previous summer. There was a strong belief that the British Army was advancing to extract revenge for the killing of their red-coated brethren. Their worry was so intense that the camp posted guards each night to watch for any English flotilla that might be coming down the lake. I was frequently asked the whereabouts of the redcoat army, all the more since the Ojibwe seemed to believe that I was gifted with the ability, by means of dreams, to have foreknowledge of the future and to therefore know of any designs of an attack. I tried to convince them that no such danger existed but had little success.

The next day, we joined in the sugar making. Our first task was to collect birch bark to make sap-collecting buckets. During the spring season, bark easily peals from the trunk in large pieces. We placed tobacco offerings at the base of the birch trees from which we stripped bark. While the women fashioned the buckets, we men busied ourselves whittling hardwood spiels that would direct the sweet sap from the tree trunk to the bucket. The spiels were made so that they had both a sap groove and a notch for hanging the buckets.

If the night had been below freezing temperatures and the morning sun warmed the leafless tree tops, the sap would rise in the tree trunks and drip into our containers. This sap was periodically collected in pails and carried to a central storage vat made of a moose skin which held about fifty gallons. Collecting the sap was the job of children who went about this chore happily despite the fact that they often had to wade through ice water puddles on the forest floor. Their spirits were buoyed by the prospect of eating their fill of maple sugar. Sometimes the women rewarded them by pouring some of the thickened syrup onto the snow to form a maple candy.

The large sap tank was located near a building containing the boiling fires which were kept roaring day and night. The sap was heated slowly in large copper kettles of ten to twenty gallons until rapidly boiling. Boiling produced foam that needed to be occasionally skimmed off and so called maple sand which had to be removed. Once the sap reached a thick consistency, it was filtered to remove the sand and transferred to a wooden granulating trough where it was worked with a paddle until it became solid sugar. Thick syrup could also be poured into wooden molds and left to harden. The resulting maple sugar cakes were later packed into *makakoon,* or bark boxes, for storage and transport.

By the end of April, the sap began to turn cloudy, and the sugaring season ended. During this time, our family produced sixteen hundred pounds of solid sugar and thirty-six gallons of syrup. Although we men occasionally hunted and fished for food when we were not gathering firewood for the boilers, as a family, we consumed at least three hundred pounds of sugar. Some families lived on nothing else during the sugaring season. *Wawatum* warned us, however, that if we ate only sugar, we would soon be "shitting like a moose." By this, I believe he meant that we would get constipated.

While we were making sugar, a tragedy occurred when a toddler fell onto a sugar boiler and was horribly scalded. Although the little girl was quickly snatched out and the entire camp participated in a curing ceremony, the child soon died, putting the entire camp into intense mourning. The child's little body was placed upon a tree scaffold until we returned to the lakeshore where the family's burial ground was located. There, a large grave was dug and carefully lined with birch bark. The girl's body was laid on the bark accompanied by an ax, a pair of snowshoes, several pairs of moccasins, a small kettle filled with meat, a string of beads, a tote strap, and a paddle, the latter two items signaling her gender. All this was covered by sheets of bark and logs placed above the burial which were also covered with bark. The hole was then filled with dirt, but none fell upon the corpse. The grave was marked by a wooden stake that bore a carving of an inverted crane which was the child's clan totem. The grieving mother had taken a lock of the child's hair, and as I endeavored to comfort her, she told me through her tears that she would take this lock with her to her own grave so that she would discover her little daughter in the afterlife. The parents of the child subsequently cut their hair and would wear raggedy clothes until a "restoring the mourners" ceremony was held sometime in the future.

The Ojibwe believe that the dead person walks the "road of the souls" to a better world populated by their ancestors. The road has perils, but those who have lived a virtuous life survive the journey with the aid of the grave goods provided at burial. In some cases, it is believed that the spirit of the dead becomes separated from the body and lingers on the earth. No matter how beloved the person may have been in life, wandering spirits are extremely malignant and very dangerous to the living.

Several days after the funeral, when we were busy repairing our canoes for the long voyage to Michilimackinac, another near disaster involving a child took place. One evening, the parents of a young boy who lived on the edge of the camp were alerted to trouble by the frantic barking of their son's small dog and the boy's cries of distress. Emerging from the wigwam, the father saw that a large panther was stalking his son. The father picked up a heavy canoe paddle and, disregarding his own safety, charged the panther which, after snarling, spitting, and batting at the paddle with his huge claws, finally turned and fled into the forest.

From time to time, panthers menaced Indian settlements, hoping to take a dog or child; and once such an attack occurred, the Indians knew the animal would likely return. For this reason, a hunt was organized for the following morning, and I was invited to join the party. The accuracy and range of my long rifle was by now well known among the Indians and, in fact, had become the object of myth. They had also seen my panther cape.

The next morning, a party of twenty hunters set out in search of the big cat, and the dogs soon picked up his trail. After a chase of only

CHARLES CLELAND

a mile, the panther was found in a tree. When we arrived, the dogs were dancing and leaping madly at the base of the tree, and their frantic barking had set the cat into a fit of snarling rage on his perch above us. Some of the hunters looked my way, expecting me to put my rifle to work, but I believed that the brave father should have the honor of the kill. In the end, it took the balls from several muskets to drop the panther to the ground. The waiting dogs swarmed the dead body too late for any real revenge against their mortal feline enemy.

Several days later, we said good-bye to our kin and, in fine weather, pushed off our canoes to retrace our journey of six months earlier. Our canoes were very heavily laden, and we were mindful to keep close to the shore. Now the trees, so splendid in their yellow and red vestments as we descended the lake, were sporting new leaves which displayed every conceivable shade of pastel green. As our canoes glided quietly through the emerald shore water, we were transfixed by the beauty of the cool, wet spring woodlands. Occasionally, deer raised their heads from drinking to watch us passing, with their white tails twitching nervously. Eagles cruising the shallows for dead fish were our constant companions overhead, and we took these sacred birds as an omen of good fortune for our journey.

We made our way past the steep, giant dunes of the "sleeping bear" and paddled northward passing streams, large and small, entering *Michigami*. After several days of paddling, we rounded a point of land to find the Grand Traverse stretching before us in the form of ten miles of open water to the opposite shore. The day, being nearly done, *Wawatum* thought it wise to postpone our crossing until the early morning calm. We followed the shoreline south into the lee of the peninsula which sheltered us from the west wind. We soon came to a substantial harbor, and entering, we encountered a camp of perhaps fifteen families. Like us, they all seemed to be returning from winter hunts with heavily laden canoes. We approached cautiously until a man, *Wawatum*, recognized by his face paint as a fellow clansman, beckoned us to come ashore. We did and found a convenient place to spend the night.

I was received with curiosity and politeness by our fellow travelers who proved to be a mixture of Ojibwe and Odawa. They, like the people in our sugar camp, were very anxious about the possibility of an impending attack by the British redcoats and, as before, believed that I might have foreknowledge of the whereabouts of the soldiers.

We also learned that among their members was a *tchissakwinni,* a "seer" who had the power to summon and consult with the spirit of the Great Turtle, a *manitou* who never tells lies. In preparation for a consultation with this spirit, the men of the camp had constructed a *tchissakan,* or "spirit lodge." This structure was built around eight sturdy ten-foot poles which were sunk two to three feet into the ground in a circle not more than five feet in diameter. Every other post had a *shishigan* attached, turtle shell containers filled with pebbles, or shot which rattle when the post is shaken. The sides are interlaced with willow branches and then covered with blankets and hides while leaving a small entrance for the *tchissakwinni.* The top of the structure was left open for the spirits to enter.

As night fell, small fires were lit around the *tchissakan* to provide light. At this point, the *tchissakwinni* appeared. He was a very old and wrinkled man who was practically naked. He entered the spirit lodge, and the door was laced shut behind him. No sooner had he entered, then the entire lodge began to shake violently and the *shishigan* to jangle loudly. These actions announced the coming of the *manitoog* or "spirits." I could also hear wheezing sounds coming from the lodge as if the spirits were out of breath after a long journey; there was also loud stomping as if the spirits had landed after jumping from a great height. There was said to be many *manidog* present in the lodge at this time as they were identified by their distinct voices. These now issued from the *tchissakan* in a cacophony including howling, barking, screaming, and sobbing as well as some fragments of articulate speech. I recognized snatches of French, English, and Ojibwe among several languages I did not recognize. The din eventually died away to a long silence that was eventually broken by a low, feeble voice which sounded much like a puppy. This voice brought cries of joy and approval from the audience since it was recognized as the voice of *Misike,* the "Turtle" spirit who speaks in a language which is unintelligible to Ojibwe speakers. Translation of the turtle's words is left to his messenger-translator who is called *Ishkabewis.*

Once these spirits were present, the people in attendance arose with questions and threw tobacco into the fires in anticipation of an answer from *Misike.* A woman asked the turtle if her husband, who was very sick, would recover his health. *Ishkabewis* translated his reply, "Yes, he would recover but only if he were treated with a root medicine called *busidjibikuguk*. A warrior then rose and posed the question on everyone's mind: "Where are the British redcoats, and will they seek revenge on the Ojibwe?" With this question, the spirit lodge shook so violently I feared it would collapse, and then all was quiet. This, I took to mean that the spirit had departed. After a short time, the Great Turtle's voice was again heard speaking in his own strange language as he delivered a long answer. I listened closely to the turtle's strange words, and I detected some familiar root words and sounds similar to those of the Ojibwe language. I concluded that the turtle was speaking a very ancient Ojibwe dialect, comparable to the use of Latin in the Catholic mass. The voice of *Ishkabewis* translated the Turtle Spirit's words and said that he had just flown over the Lake of the Hurons and beyond to Montréal and had seen no soldiers, but then returning by way of the Saint Lawrence River, he had found the river to be covered with many boats containing many, many redcoat soldiers bound for the west to make war on the Indians.

The warrior then asked if they could avert a war by visiting Sir William Johnson, the British Indian agent at Fort Niagara. "Yes," said the turtle. "He will not only receive you as friends but will fill your canoes with presents." This response brought a great sigh of relief from the crowd, and their anxiety was quickly lifted as various people cried out that they would make the trip to Fort Niagara.

Several other people asked questions of the Turtle Spirit on a variety of subjects. The answers were so positive and detailed that I could not refrain from asking my own question, even though I could not help but notice that the turtle's answers always left room for a wide interpretation. I put some tobacco on the fire and asked if I would ever again revisit my native country. The spirit lodge shook as usual, and the turtle's response was translated by his helper. He said, "You should take courage, since nothing will happen to hurt you, and you will see your countrymen again and talk to your kin." This expression wrought so strongly on my gratitude that I presented an additional large offering of tobacco.

CHAPTER 14

WE BEGAN THE Grand Traverse on an early June morning with barely a ripple on the glossy blue surface of the Grand Traverse Bay. Before we were halfway across, however, a stiff wind blew in from *Michigami,* and we were soon fighting three-foot following waves. Although such a sea hastened our crossing, it also posed serious risks. Since our heavily laden canoes were anything but agile, there was a danger that a large wave might swing the stern of our canoes broadside to the waves while the bow was caught in a trough. Such a situation would likely roll the canoe. Under these conditions, the stern paddler had to be acutely aware of the size and position of each incoming wave and to steer the canoe obliquely to the wave crests.

With *Wawatum* and *Miigwan's* paddling skills much in evidence, we managed to reach the shore safely, where we paused to rest and offer a prayer of thanks before following the coast northward. Although we were somewhat under the lee of the Fox Islands, the waves continued to build during the morning, and we finally decided to camp soon after midday. We put ashore on a sandy beach just north of a very small island located close to the shore. Our camp was beside a small but swift stream where there were signs of several previous Indian camps. Judging by the substantial litter of sucker bones scattered about, we surmised that this stream must have a heavy spring spawning run of that species which drew Indian fishermen.

While the rest of the family spent the afternoon exploring the high sandy ridges which paralleled the shore in this area in hope of finding mushrooms, I decided to ponder my future while watching the breakers rolling in on the beach. A major object of my western venture was to establish myself as a fur trade merchant. This venture had had both ups and downs. I had learned the trade and been successful in gathering furs and selling these on the Montréal market for a good profit, but I had also lost all my goods and stored furs in the Indian attack on Fort

Michilimackinac the previous summer. This was a major financial setback to my economic welfare. Naturally, I am happy to have escaped with my life, but I am now reduced to the lowest rung of the fur trade ladder, that as a collector of furs on credit. While my labor during the winter would provide me with a temporary means of support, I could not easily acquire or trade goods, except by going to Montréal where I had to reestablish my credit and my partnership with M. Etienne Campion.

I feel I am on the verge of an important decision. After returning to Michilimackinac, I could remain with my Indian family as a fur trapper, return to New Jersey and take up farming, or go to Montréal and try to renew my fur trade business and contacts. While these options had various degrees of appeal, as it turned out, I would not do any of them in the near term. One thing I did decide was that my curiosity about the wilderness country and its native people still had strong attractions for me.

That evening, we gathered around a fire on the beach; and as the wind dropped and calm was restored to the lake, we enjoyed a lingering sunset and the long, long twilight, which is a special part of northern summers. This was the time I chose to tell my Indian family that I would soon, but reluctantly, be leaving their company.

Several days later, we rounded *Waugoshance* Point and entered the rambunctious Straits of Mackinac. When we reached the small wharf in front of the water-gate of the fort, we were surprised to see that there were no British soldiers, practically no Indians and very few Canadian traders in residence. This scene was in sharp contrast to the usual situation of early summer when many hundreds of Indians and traders were camped around the fort. In normal times, voyagers and fur merchants would be arriving from far and wide, and the fort grounds would be loud with laughter, music, and every kind of entertainment. The silence we witnessed now was the aftermath of the events of the previous summer. British merchants feared the Indians, and the Indians feared the British Army.

Over the next several days, *Wawatum*, *Miigwan*, and I bargained with the few traders in residence for the furs, hides, dried meat, oil, and maple sugar that we had collected over the winter months. We paid our debts to several traders and divided our remaining assets into five parts. My fifth consisted of one hundred beaver pelts, sixty raccoon skins, and six otter skins—all for an equivalent value of one hundred and sixty dollars. With these profits, I traded for several shirts, pantaloons, a blanket, leggings, and sacks of ammunition and tobacco. To the use of the latter, I had become much addicted during the long winter.

My life remained tranquil and happy as I became reacquainted with my friends among the Indians and voyagers and with the conveniences of civilized life. Here, I refer to such wonderful inventions such as the privy, chairs, and woven clothing. My tranquility was abruptly ended when on the eighth day after our return, two canoes of Saginaw Chippewa arrived. They had recently been involved with the ongoing siege of Detroit. Recognizing me as an Englishman, they quickly determined to kill me. In this, they were abetted by my old nemesis, *Wenniway*, who was still living in the environs of the fort. Despite the persuasions of my friends and acquaintances to spare me, the Saginaw warriors persisted in insisting that I must be killed.

I decided to lay low for the time being and to avoid the Saginaw warriors and *Wenniway*. While hiding out, I began to think about an idea which had been in the back of my mind for some time. If I could get back into the fur trade, I would like to have a new location that reduced direct competition with the many traders congregated near the fort, and that would be more attractive to my Indian customers who are uncomfortable in the presence of the British Army that I was sure would soon reoccupy the fort. Toward this end, I considered several locations including Odawa Island and Round Island. Since Round Island is located in the Straits of Mackinac, and therefore, quite close, I decided to visit it.

Round Island is located between Mackinac Island and Bois Blanc Island and is only about two miles long and three quarters of a mile wide. Although it is currently uninhabited, it is handy to a large *metis* community on Mackinac Island as well as a very large Indian fishing village on the most western tip of Bois Blanc Island. I decided to explore it in order to assess its suitability for my needs as well as to get me out of the environs of Michilimackinac for a day. Little did I know that this trip would result in a horrific experience!

I set off by myself early in the morning to visit the island which is only seven miles across the water from Fort Michilimackinac. In due course, I reached the island and beached my small canoe without incident. I discovered that Round Island has a coastal as well as an

CHARLES CLELAND

upland region. The latter, in the center of the island, is dominated by magnificent stands of huge old maple trees, while the coastal plain has a mixture of hardwoods as well as plentiful cedars which prefer its moist soil. The lowland forests are draped with long strands of lichen hanging from boughs, while tree trunks are covered with rich growths of moss and lichens reflecting the wet, foggy conditions that often prevail over the Straits of Mackinac. These conditions create an eerie environment even on a bright sunny day.

As I was making my way around the island looking for a suitable place to site a trading establishment, I suddenly had the uneasy feeling that I was being watched. Most woodsmen know this feeling, but none can explain it; perhaps it comes from a subconscious awareness of another's presence. At any rate, my suspicion alone gave rise to an added awareness on my part as well as a feeling of nervous anticipation. Alerted, I turned my attention to my immediate surroundings, conscious of all sounds and movements. I ceased movement to focus my senses. During hunting excursions in company of *Wawatum* and *Miigwan,* I had been schooled in many aspects of woodcraft; and after months of training, they both told me I was a decent tracker, for an Englishman.

Nonetheless, while the feeling of being observed persisted, and although I could not immediately detect any source of danger, I moved away from my direction of travel being very careful not to leave signs of my passage. I soon found a low ridge where I could observe my back trail from a hidden position. I remained there motionless for a considerable period of time. For if *Wawatum* had taught me anything, it was that a good hunter must be patient, and I was now a hunter.

The woods around my hiding spot were shaded by mature trees so there was very little undergrowth, and I could see for quite some distance. I soon realized that the small birds which had begun to call and sing since I had hidden myself suddenly went quiet. At the same time, I saw movement on my back trail. I focused a small telescope I always carried and was able to make out a man moving slowly and studying the ground. He was very clearly tracking me. When he got to the place where I had left my trail, he began to range back and forth looking for signs. He had lost me. As I watched, I suddenly realized he was familiar to me; and when he entered a small patch of sunlight, I recognized him immediately; he was none other than my enemy, *Wenniway.*

I was being followed by a man who had twice tried to kill me and who had advocated killing me only a few days before. I was convinced that this was the reason he had followed me to this deserted island. With this thought in mind, I slowly raised my Pennsylvania rifle and took careful aim. As I was about to squeeze the trigger, several doubts stilled my finger.

Although I had witnessed much killing both by soldiers at Fort Levi and by Indians at Fort Michilimackinac, I had never actually killed anyone myself, and I found this prospect abhorrent. Second, if I killed *Wenniway* and this fact became known, I would set off a blood feud between *Wenniway* and *Wawatum's* relatives which could last for generations and would likely result in the deaths of many innocents. I decided to bide my time.

Wenniway soon disappeared in the brush, and I decided my best option was to track him so I would know his whereabouts. Although my first instinct was to get up and quickly follow him, *Wawatum's* good advice again prevailed, and I waited. After about a half an hour, I slowly made my way to the place where I had last seen him, and I soon picked up the subtle signs of his passing.

The art of tracking depends upon the ability to notice slight disturbances to your surroundings, and accordingly, I soon saw a bent fern frond and, further along, a partial moccasin track in a wet spot and then a little later a freshly broken, dead cedar twig. By following such clues, I followed his trail, and two things soon became apparent. First, he was making little effort to hide his movements; and second, he was headed for the place I had left my canoe. The thought occurred to me that *Wenniway* was probably setting an ambush for me when I returned to my canoe.

I had barely had this thought when I heard a distant gunshot from the direction in which I had been tracking *Wenniway*. Mystified, I continued tracking ever so slowly and cautiously. Finally, I could see the lake through the trees, and I carefully crawled to a spot where I could see up and down the beach without revealing myself. I saw my canoe and a short distance away another, which must have brought *Wenniway* to the island. Nearby, there was a dead moose on the beach which must have been killed by *Wenniway* who was busy butchering it. He had already piled much meat into his canoe.

CHARLES CLELAND

The thought now occurred to me that maybe *Wenniway* had come to Round Island to hunt. However, thinking this idea over, it seemed unlikely since his canoe was so near mine and because I found him clearly following my trail. Perhaps when he lost my trail, he decided to leave the island before I discovered him and had the chance to turn the tables; but before he left, he encountered the young moose so near his canoe that he couldn't resist killing it.

I now determined to confront him, and I moved out onto the beach into his clear view perhaps one hundred feet away and walked toward him. *Wenniway* saw me immediately and ran to his canoe, pushed off, and began paddling furiously toward deeper water. I, likewise, ran to my canoe and followed him. We were both making our best speed, but lacking a load and riding much higher in the water, I was moving faster. Even so, it was fifteen minutes until I drew abreast of him, and *Wenniway* realized he could not outrun me. He let his canoe drift and sat, panting from exertion, and then he turned toward me.

I approached to within twenty feet or perhaps less, when *Wenniway* suddenly threw up his musket and pointed it directly at my face and pulled the trigger. In that instance, I believed I was a dead man. Just then, I heard a metallic click. He had not reloaded his gun after killing the moose. For a second or two, that empty sound hung in the air, but now my mortal terror had been transformed into pure rage. This rage fled my body in the form of an involuntary roar. By reflex alone, my rifle came up, and I discharged a load of heavy swan shot into the water line of *Wenniway*'s canoe. I saw pieces of birch bark and water erupting in all directions. Water was gushing into a gaping hole, and under the weight of the moose meat, the canoe was rapidly sinking. *Wenninway*, who apparently could not swim, began to scream, alternately begging for mercy and calling me a devil spirit. I picked up my paddle and paddled toward the fort and did not look back. *Wenniway*'s screams died in a sputtering gurgle as the lake swallowed him.

After returning to *Wawatum*'s lodge, I told no one of my fateful meeting with *Wenniway*. A few days later, I heard the rumor that his body had washed up on Bois Blanc Island, apparently the result of an encounter with an underwater demon.

Although *Wenniway* was gone, the Saginaw Indians were still in the vicinity and still wished me dead. I decided I would flee, and *Wawatum* was determined to see me safely away from Michilimackinac. In the company of my family, we crossed the Straits to Point Saint Ignace and then on eastward to the scattering of small islands called Les Cheneaux. Here, we had a discussion concerning our destination, and *Wawatum* suggested Odawa Island. I agreed since it was not only near at hand but was also a place I wanted to consider as a possible location for a future trading establishment. As *Wawatum* wanted to hunt on the island, we needed to get the permission from the headman of the Odawa band now frequenting the place. As fortune would have it, the headman whose name was *Aamoo*, the "Bee," was a boyhood friend of *Wawatum*. *Aamoo's* father was Ojibwe but his mother Odawa. When his mother was killed, his father married *Aamoo's* mother's younger sister, and they moved to Odawa Island. Although *Aamoo* was a clan brother of *Wawatum* by birth, he was otherwise raised among the Odawa and spoke their dialect of the language. The next day, our family paddled east along the north shore of Lake Huron until we entered the Detour passage, and Odawa Island lay close on our right. We followed its coast north and east, first crossing a large bay until we came to a group of small islands opposite the mouth of another bay which was narrow but deep. The Potagannissing River had its mouth at the end of this bay, and on its north bank near the mouth of the river was the summer village of the Odawa band that claimed the island.

There were but four wigwams on the site when we arrived, but the surrounding coastal area was covered by gardens and orchards. We stood off from the shore until several armed warriors looked us over and, deciding we posed no threat, bid us to land.

On several occasions I had heard *Wawatum* describe the Odawa dialect as sounding as if the speaker were speaking Ojibwe with his mouth full of soup. He could demonstrate this observation with several stock phrases, which never ceased to produce a laugh. As our Odawa hosts greeted us, I could clearly hear the soup quality of their accent and had to suppress a smile when my eyes met *Miigwan's*. *Wawatum* inquired as to the whereabouts of *Aamoo*, and we were informed that he was on one of the offshore islands fishing but would return later in the day. Learning of the relationship between *Aamoo* and *Wawatum* and our intentions, we were invited to assemble our lodge and to await his return. As we waited, our dog waged a war with the locals, and despite repeated attempts by *Miigwan*, me, and several Odawa boys who waded into the snarling pack with stout clubs hitting dogs right and left, our efforts only resulted in temporary truces.

Finally, in the early evening, *Aamoo* returned. He had only caught a few small catfish and was disgusted. Nevertheless, he and *Wawatum* greeted each other with enthusiasm, and we were invited to his lodge for a meal. Despite his hospitality, *Aamoo* appeared to be well named. He was a small but very active man with a sharp tongue. After a good meal of corn soup and a pipe had been smoked and small gifts exchanged, *Wawatum* asked permission for us to camp and hunt on Odawa Island for a few days. Specifically, *Wawatum* wanted to visit the marsh at the head of the Potagannissing River, which he had heard was a place of plentiful game. *Aamoo* readily agreed, on the condition that he accompanying us as a guide. When *Wawatum* replied that we could guide ourselves, *Aamoo* retorted, "If you do not have a guide, you will be wading around in the marsh until the snow falls, and then I and my men will have to come and rescue you." This response was accompanied by good-natured kidding and storytelling between the two old friends. Finally, *Wawatum* admitted that he would have been disappointed if *Aamoo* could not accompany us.

Rather than going with us on the hunting trip, *Wabigonkwe* and *Anangons* decided to stay in camp and repair our wall and floor mats that were beginning to show much wear. *Wawatum, Miigwan, Aamoo,* and I set off in two canoes up the Potagannissing River, which proved to be a small fast stream above its mouth. A mile or so up river, however, the land flattened into a huge water filled basin. As we proceeded, the river's course became less and less distinct as it braided its way through a seemingly endless jungle of cattails. Given that the marsh vegetation towered over our canoes, our visibility was so limited; it was difficult to follow the main channel and, was, indeed, a place to get lost.

The marsh itself was a natural wonderland filled with ducks and geese and legions of red winged blackbirds who screeched at us from their cattail perches. Overhead ospreys and eagles patrolled the basin, occasionally engaging in aerial dogfights over dead fish. The water was clear and shallow, allowing us to observe many species of small fish as they darted away from our passing canoes.

As we traveled upriver, the channel was blocked by many small beaver dams. Every several hundred yards, we were forced to get out of our canoes, stand on top of the dam, and then lift the canoes and place them on the upriver side of the dam. We could then reload our vessels and proceed.

On several occasions, the river swung near wooded banks, and we set up our evening camp on such a place located only a few feet above the water. Exploring the area, we saw signs of beaver, muskrats, otter, and the tracks of moose and bear. We also discovered the flint chips and sherds of fired earthen pottery left behind by ancient campers who, like us, must have found this site as inviting and, no doubt, with as many mosquitoes.

The next morning, we moved on; and before long, we sighted wooded highlands to the north and west. As we approached the hills, the river narrowed and flowed from a valley where it connected a series of four small lakes. On our way up the river, we were all immersed in the beauty and abundance of the country and were all relaxed and full of enjoyment. There was, however, one incident which added some excitement to our lives that day.

We had decided to hunt and were proceeding quietly and slowly upriver; *Aamoo* and *Miigwan* were in the lead canoe and *Wawatum* and I in the other. Arriving at the third lake, little more than a wide spot in the river, we saw a bull-moose standing belly deep in the water, feeding on water lilies. Alerted to our unexpected presence, it moved to the shore and stood with its nose raised, trying to scent us.

Miigwan, who was in the bow of the first canoe, took aim and fired. The moose jumped straight up and collapsed in a heap where he had stood. My guess was that *Miigwan*'s ball had hit either his brain or spine. We paddled up to the dead moose and disembarked from the canoes. While *Miigwan* reloaded his musket, we all congratulated him on his fine shooting. While we were standing around the moose remarking on his size and magnificent rack, he suddenly twitched and jumped to his feet. We learned later that *Miigwan*'s shot had squarely struck the base of one of the moose's antlers and had merely stunned the beast. An angry bull moose is not to be taken lightly, and we found ourselves only a few feet away from one that was totally enraged. *Aamoo* shouted *bimibatoon* or "run." We needed no urging, and we scattered like a flock of chickens in the presence of a hawk. All of us, except *Miigwan*, had left our firearms in the canoes, and we all quickly found safety by climbing trees. *Miigwan*, however, could not climb with the gun in his hand, so the angry moose was soon intent on chasing him alone. *Miigwan* desperately darted from tree to tree trying to get off another shot. Finally, the moose stopped, and *Miigwan* jumped out from behind a huge old maple tree and shot the animal at point-blank range. This time, it was truly dead; and for the second time that day, we congratulated *Miigwan* for killing the same moose.

We spent most of the rest of the day skinning and butchering the moose and camping at that spot that night. Our dinner was made up of moose delicacies such as the tongue, liver, and eye balls. The next day, we headed back to the river mouth and our base camp. Going over the many beaver dams as we went downstream was now much more difficult and strenuous, since we had to unload and reload hundreds of pounds of meat from each canoe at each dam. When we finally arrived back at camp, the women immediately been began cutting the meat into strips for drying, and *Wabigonkwe* noted that the thick moose hide would make good moccasins and winter boots.

Over the years I have spent in the wilderness, I remained in tolerably good health despite exposure to all manner of hardships. That all changed, however, when we returned to our camp on Potagannissing Bay where I developed a cough and a severe headache, and I found myself feeling very weak and exhausted. After a few days, I began to ache all over, and my throat was so sore I could hardly swallow. Most fearful, however, I developed a very high fever and the flux.

Wabigonkwe took charge of my treatment and declared that she had seen this kind of fever in the past. *Wawatum* hovered near and said that my condition had one or two causes, either I had offended the spirits of an "other than human" person by bad hunting practices; or more likely, I was the victim of an evil spell of an unknown shaman. In either case, he said, my sickness was caused by a foreign object that had entered my body; and in order to return to good health, the offending object must be removed.

In the meantime, *Wabigonkwe* insisted that I drink much water and a tea that was an infusion made from needles of the *shingob* or balsam fir tree. This drink did ease my sore throat. She also set a small bowl near my head containing dried leaves of the bearberry plant called by the Ojibwe, *miskwaabiimag*. These leaves were smudged to produce a cloud of smoke which soon relieved my headache. *Wabigonkwe* also prepared an infusion made of the bark of the winterberry shrub, which she insisted I drink to control my flux. Unfortunately, it did not stop my frequent trips to my toilet area behind the *wigwam*.

It must be said that the Ojibwe have an immense knowledge of the healing qualities of hundreds, if not thousands of plants. This knowledge far exceeds the medicines prepared by the physicians of my native New Jersey, who were part barbers, tooth pullers, and herbalists. This having been said, although *Wabigokwe*'s medicines relieved some of my symptoms, they did not cure my illness. In fact, I was becoming progressively weaker and wasted. After several weeks, a red rash appeared on my chest and back, and my fever was so high that it gave me wild dreams. At this point, *Wawatum* sent *Miigwan* to the mainland to find an Ojibwe village in order to fetch a *nanandawi*, a shaman who is able to cure by sucking. The Canadians refer to such doctors as *jongleurs* or jugglers.

The next day, the *nanandawi,* a very old wizard of a man, arrived at my sick bed. He placed a bowl of water on a new blanket, and in the water were three hollow bones about four inches long. The *nanandawi* darkened the wigwam and proceeded to summon the healing energies of the *manitouk* by singing, dancing and wild gesticulations, all the while shaking his rattle. This is called *manitou kazo* or "talking to the spirits" to invoke their power in order to establish a special relationship between the spirits and the patient.

Eventually, the *nanandawi* took one of the bones out of the bowl of water. In so doing, he did not use his fingers, but the bone appeared to jump into his mouth as he leaned over the bowl. Now he applied one end of the bone to my chest, and he sucked strongly on the other. After a time, he suddenly seemed to force the bone into his mouth and to swallow it, which seemed to cause him great pain. Soon he recovered and repeated the process with the second bone. After this, he went back to singing and then began to retch until he vomited one of the bones which he passed around for inspection, but we found nothing remarkable about this bone. A while later, he threw up the other bone; and on this one, there was a small groove which contained a white substance that looked like a piece of a feather quill. The *nanandawi* declared that this was the thing which had caused of my sickness, and he destroyed it by throwing it in the fire. The curing ceremony was thus concluded, and *Wawatum* paid the *nanandawi* handsomely for his services.

CHARLES CLELAND

After this treatment, I began to feel a bit better each day, and all my symptoms gradually disappeared. Nonetheless, *Wabigonkwe* insisted that I continue to drink her foul-smelling herbal concoctions for another month.

While in the throes of the fever, I had many dreams, which *Wawatum* said were especially potent, since my spirit was on the verge of leaving my body for good. It is in this state, he said, that divine revelations come to dreamers and that these dreams are undoubtedly true. In this regard, I did have several dreams in which I was back in my boyhood home, which I sensed to be safe and secure. In the most dramatic of these dreams, I was in my warm bed in the loft of our cabin; and as I looked out through my crack in the chinking, I could see my father and myself happily going about our farm chores. As I watched this blissful scene, I saw myself rapidly change into my present self. I became tall and strong. I was wearing beaded moccasins and a leather shirt; my hair was long, and my white stripe was clearly visible. My face was painted with a single red stripe across the bridge of my nose and under my eyes, and my long rifle was in my hand. My father turned and looked at me, and I could see fear in his eyes. He did not recognize me, perhaps taking me for an Indian.

A feeling of desolation swept over me as I realized that my life on the wilderness frontier had slowly and imperceptibly molded me into a very different person from the farm boy who had set off on an adventure only a few years before. That new person I had become could never go home.

When I had sufficiently recovered my health, I also regained my fear of being discovered by the Saginaw warriors. *Wawatum* thought it best to leave Odawa Island and to cross the DeTour passage and to camp among the Les Cheneaux Islands. We did so, and even though our camp was on a secluded bay of Lake Huron, it was also near the main east-west travel route between Michilimackinac and Montréal, and I felt uneasy about the possibility of being discovered.

I spent the next several days at this camp perched near the top of the huge old pine tree, where I had a good view down the lakeshore toward the Straits of Mackinac. In this manner, I could be forewarned of any pursuit by the villains from Saginaw. On the third day of my vigil, I spotted a canoe with the sail headed our way from the direction of Michilimackinac. Eventually, I determined from the shape of the sail and the manner that the canoe was being paddled that its occupants were Canadians rather than Indian. Thinking they might be bound for Montréal, I went to the shore as they drew abreast and bid them land. As they approached, I was surprised and pleased to recognize Madame Cadotte, an Ojibwe woman better known to me as *Athanasius*. She was my former Ojibwe language teacher and was being escorted by three Canadians who were taking her home to the Sault. *Athanasius*, is a large woman, perhaps about twenty-five years old, and she had already born Jean-Baptiste four children. She was as glad to see me as I was to see her, and she invited me to join her on her trip. Knowing that her husband had the means to protect me from my Indian enemies, I readily accepted her invitation.

My departure for the Sault meant that I would have to take my leave of my Indian family, at least for the foreseeable future. This was a difficult parting for everyone. My old mother, *Wabigonkwe,* and *Anangons* wept and hugged me so tight I nearly lost my breath, and my brother, *Miigwan,* was also overcome with emotion and kept telling me how much he would miss my companionship. For his part, *Wawatum,* both my father and friend, kept up a steady stream of blessings and prayers to the *manidogs* asking that my journey be safe and that I be returned to the family very soon. As fate would have it, I would not see them again for full year; and by then, my little niece, *Papakin,* would be two years old.

Reaching the Sault two days later, I was overjoyed to see my old friend and benefactor Jean-Baptiste Cadotte. Our reunion, as in the case of my return to Fort Michilimackinac, was short-lived and for the same reason. Six days after our arrival at the Sault, a party of fifteen Ojibwe warriors from the Straits area led by *Mahgekewis* the chief who had carried out the attack on the fort, arrived at the Cadottes' door. Yet again, I found myself hiding in a garret. This time, however, hiding was of no avail because the Indians knew perfectly well that I was the guest of the Cadottes. Jean-Baptiste strongly vouched for me and such was his and his wife's standing among the Ojibwe that *Mahgekewis* agreed to leave me in peace.

While *Mahgekewis* and his men were still at the Sault visiting with the resident Ojibwe of the crane clan, a messenger arrived with an invitation from Sir William Johnson, the king's Indian agent for the Ojibwe to attend a peace conference to be held at Fort Niagara located at the western end of Lake Ontario. *Mahgekewis* was anxious to go and to leave immediately. It occurred to me that if I could accompany this delegation to Niagara, I would likely be safely transported halfway to Montréal. I consulted with Jean-Baptiste about this plan, and although these warriors had recently demonstrated that they wanted to take my life, we believed that if *Mahgekewis* would take me under his protection, I would be fairly safe. Consequently, we met with *Mahgekewis,* and in exchange for supplies for his trip, he agreed to see me safely to Fort Niagara. M. Cadotte supplied the presents from his trade store, and *Mahgekewis* distributed them to his warriors, thus further establishing himself as a generous provider for his followers.

Soon I bid the Cadottes good-bye and departed with *Mahgekewis* and his fighting men for Niagara. Rather than risk going south down Lake Huron to the Detroit River and into Lake Erie to reach our objective, *Mahgekewis* decided it was wiser to give Detroit a wide berth since it was still under siege by Pontiac's warriors. Instead, we would take a little used shortcut to the east.

We coasted along the north shore of Lake Huron to its east shore until we reached a huge bay that is separated by a large peninsula from the main body of the lake. Along this entire coast, we found village after village with only women and children in residence. We were informed that their men had gone to Niagara. Finally, we reached a large bay known to the Indians as *Nottawasaga,* where we entered a river by the same name and then a small creek until we reached a portage. Carrying our baggage and the canoes, we walked nine miles to Lac Aux Claires known to me in later years as Lake Simco. We paddled down the main body of the lake until we ultimately reached the southern end, where we found a trail that led south to Fort Toranto on Lake Ontario, forty miles away.

We cached our canoes and began the long portage to Lake Ontario. I was loaded with a pack which weighed well over one hundred pounds, and I noticed several of my Indian companions smiling as I shouldered the burden. Not only had they assigned me the task of a woman, they also clearly did not believe I could carry such a heavy weight for long. What they did not know was that the hard-carrying I had done in moving our camp at winter's end had conditioned me for such tasks.

The warriors set off down the trail in the usual Indian traveling pace, a rolling gait, half fast walk and half slow trot. They could and did keep up this ground-eating pace for hours on end. The trail was narrow and, since it had been raining, very muddy. The hot and humid weather brought out hordes of mosquitoes and black flies. Unfortunately, my burden limited my ability to swat these insects away, and I suffered greatly. Eventually we reached the old French fur post of Fort Toranto where we paused for two days to build canoes.

My companions cut down two large elm trees and stripped off the bark in single pieces, both eighteen feet in length. The bark was then outfitted with a few ribs and struts, and the ends were sewn up and caulked. These new canoes carried us—eight men in one and nine in the other—down the western end of Lake Ontario to the outlet of the Niagara River. Here, we found our destination, Fort Niagara, situated at its mouth on the south bank.

Mahgekewis and his men were still uneasy at the prospect of meeting inside a British fort, so we camped short of our objective in order to reinforce their courage. In the morning, the warriors painted themselves and donned their regalia, and we solemnly entered the fort. We were immediately received by Sir William Johnson, who greeted us with a good deal of flattery in praising the power and wisdom of the great Ojibwe people.

CHARLES CLELAND

CHAPTER 15

S IR WILLIAM JOHNSON had a long face, though not by any
means gaunt. His eyes were intelligent and observant and his
nose prominent. He wore a fine jacket of green broadcloth and white
leggings, and befitting His Majesty's Indian agent, he wore a shining
silver gorget at his throat over a white stock tie. Sir William spoke with
a lilt in his voice betraying his Irish origins. His wife Molly Brant, a
matron of the Mohawk tribe, along with his own gift of oratory and
diplomacy, accounted for his huge influence among the five tribes of
the Iroquois Confederacy. Although he had once traveled west to visit
the tribes in the Detroit area, he confessed that he knew little of the
Algonquian people of the Upper Lakes country. He expressed himself
well satisfied that the Ojibwe and Odawa were well represented at this
peace conference.

Learning that I spoke their language and had become familiar
with their culture, he spent many hours questioning me concerning
the manners, customs, and attitudes of the Northern Indians. During
these conversations, I learned that Johnson was an important architect
of the new British trade policy, especially requiring the Indians to bring
their furs to one of only a few strong British military posts to trade. I
told him in no uncertain terms that this policy was a real hardship on
the Indians who had to interrupt their seasonal subsistence activities
to travel great distances in order to obtain essential supplies in trade. I
also pointed out that the concentrations of traders at these posts made it
more likely that the Indians would be cheated by unscrupulous traders.
Finally, I told him that returning to the French trade system of licensed
traders that the Indians got to know since they did business in Indian
villages was a much better system. Frankly, my comments seemed to
fall on deaf ears.

During the months of June and July, Indians from both the lower
and upper Great Lakes regions continued to arrive at Fort Niagara

for Sir William's peace conference. Considering that the Upper Lake Indians and the Iroquois are mortal enemies, I was amazed that serious hostilities had not broken out; the fact that it had not could only be a tribute to Sir William's skill as a moderator. At this same time, I was summoned to a meeting with Gen. John Bradstreet who, with a force of three thousand men, was preparing to embark for Detroit in order to lift Pontiac's siege, which had by now stretched on for an entire year. Having heard of my experience from Sir William, he offered to have me accompany his expeditionary force as a guide and as a commander of Indians scouts. After Detroit was relieved, he would send troops to reoccupy the other forts taken by the Indians the previous summer, and I would accompany these troops to Fort Michilimackinac. I begged time to consider his proposition because I still planned to visit Montréal. The general gave me a single week to decide.

By strange coincidence, an event occurred that settled my future. I decided to take a short trip to Niagara Falls which, with its roar and swirling mist, evoked the unimaginable power of nature as the water plunges over a great ledge of rock into the maelstrom below. After visiting the falls, I went to Fort Sclausser, a post on the Niagara River above the great falls to seek accommodations for the night. I found the fort crowded with a large contingent of men of the Sixtieth Regiment— the Royal Americans—a regiment of the British Army made up of colonial recruits. Everywhere I went, I could hear their young voices speaking with the accents of many of the colonies. They were entirely comfortable with each other joking, singing, and bantering in good humor. Suddenly it occurred to me that these men were like me; indeed they were my countrymen in a way that an Englishmen could never be. We were all truly Americans.

The next morning as I was walking across the parade ground, I heard someone call my name. I turned to find myself facing a tall, thin soldier in the uniform of the Royal Americans. He smiled broadly and said, "Don't you recognize me, cousin? I am Ben Henry's son, Collin, your own cousin."

I was momentarily shocked by the soldier's revelation. "Why yes," I finally stammered. "I see the family resemblance. I guess I haven't seen you for four years. How old were you when I left New Jersey?"

CHARLES CLELAND

"Just thirteen when you lit out for the wilderness, Cousin Alex. Unfortunately, I am due for guard duty in a moment. Can we get together tonight?"

"Of course, Collin, I'm anxious to hear about you, your father and brothers, and the other news from back home."

As Collin walked away, I suddenly remembered the words of the Ojibwe seer. "Don't fear. You will be among your countrymen again and will talk to your kin." His predictions had come true but just not in the same way I had imagined.

The next morning, Collin and I met for a breakfast of hard tack and black coffee. While we were eating, I took stock of my newfound cousin. He was tall and quite handsome, favoring his father. His was a pleasant countenance, and his face and arms were well tanned from outdoor living. Likewise, he looked to be fit with hard, stringy muscles. I also noted that his uniform was fairly clean and in good order, indicating that he had taken to military discipline.

"What's the news from home?" I asked.

"Last I heard was a month or so ago. Pa got hisself squeezed against a stall wall by our big Belgian—you remember Danny—a real brute. At any rate, he got two ribs stowed in. My elder brother Stephen is doing most of the work till Pa mends."

"Well, your Pa is a tough nut, and I know he will be as good as new soon. How old is Stephen now?" I inquired.

Collin thought for a second and replied, "He is two years older than I, which makes him twenty-two. By the way, Stevie has a sweetheart, that Johansen girl from town. I guess they will be getting married soon enough."

"What else is happening back home in New Jersey?"

"Well, I hear that the crops are good this year. Oh yeah, and old Mrs. Tilson who ran the general store in Wyckoff died this spring, but I can't think of much else."

"Do the folks at home hear much about the new taxes that Parliament has levied against the colonies?" I asked.

"Oh yes, in my letters from Stevie, he said that there is much talk about unfair taxes which were imposed on us without our say so. Folks are really riled up."

"How about you, Collin? How do you come to be wearing the uniform in His Majesty's army?"

"Well, it's a long story," he said with a slight frown. "As I see it, when Stevie gets married and starts his own family, he will probably inherit the farm, so I don't see much of a future for me there. I thought of taking up a trade, but I didn't want to spend several years as an apprentice earning a pittance and found, to be honest, Cousin Alex, you've always been my model going off like you did to a life in the unknown. I've always dreamed of the frontier and a life of adventure. That's why I took the king's schilling and joined up with the Royal American Regiment so I could see new country and fight the savages. Do you think you could teach me to be a fur trader once my enlistment ends? Perhaps we could be partners someday. But tell me about yourself, Cousin Alex. I know the family will be anxious to hear of you after so many years."

So at this point, I gave my young kinsman a brief history of my life as a fur merchant at Fort Michilimackinac and, before that, my travels to Albany and Montréal, my business as a sutler, and I told of my canoe voyage to the upper Great Lakes. I also told him of the attack on the fort, my narrow escape, my captivity, and my adoption into the *Wawatum* family. I concluded by noting that I had lost all my goods and pelts in the attack and was currently at loose ends and trying to find a way to restart my business by going to Montréal.

Collin was excited to hear of my many narrow escapes and my descriptions of the wonderful country I had seen.

"But aren't you headed in the wrong direction, if you're going to Montreal? Why are you headed for Detroit?"

"Yes," I replied, "but I have an offer from General Bradstreet that I didn't want to turn down. After Detroit, I will head back east again. I would be glad to help you get started in the beaver trade once I get my own business in order. In the meantime, I hope you and your companions won't be killing off all my customers for no other reason than you think they are savages. I know these people fairly well, Collin, and they have the same basic needs and desires as you and me. The Ojibwe and Odawa people need to find food, shelter, and clothing, and they want to support their families and to protect them from enemies. As I told you, I have an adopted Indian family, and I love and admire each one of them. If you are going to be a fur trader, you can't live and work with people you despise, so the first thing you need to do is to get to know some Indians. I think you will find that they are no more savages than the Englishmen who live on the frontier."

"Well, thanks for the talk, Cousin Alex. Since we are both heading for Detroit, we may meet again on the road."

"I would like that, Collin. It was a pleasure to see you again and don't forget to give my greetings to your father when you write home."

In mid-July, General Bradstreet embarked from Fort Niagara with the force of fifteen hundred redcoats. We marched to Fort Schausser where more men joined our force, including several hundred Canadians and Indians. I was appointed by the general to lead the so-called Indian battalion. We embarked from Fort Schausser in sixty longboats, each holding approximately twenty-five men and their baggage. We rowed up the river to Fort Erie, which serves as the supply depot and port for passage between eastern Lake Erie and the upper Great Lakes. Before we left this place, almost all the members of my Indian battalion deserted, having no use for either military discipline or a fight with their kinsmen around Detroit. My short experience as a leader of men was an utter failure.

We proceeded along the south coast of Lake Erie and, on the fifth day, entered Presque Isle Bay. Once we reached the head of the bay, we discovered we were trapped and had either to retrace our route to Lake Erie or to drag our boats over a narrow sandy peninsula to regain the lake. The general chose the latter option, which not only took considerable labor on our part but also badly strained the timbers of our longboats, causing subsequent leaks. Continuing west, we presently came to Sandusky Bay, which is a very shallow water body surrounded by extensive marshes. It was suggested that we pause here and send part of our force against the Miami Indian villages located to the south, but after a conference with his officers, Bradstreet ordered us to proceed to Detroit. We hoped that news of the approach of our large army would scatter Pontiac's warriors. With this goal in mind, we rowed past the mouth of the Maumee River and then north to the broad estuary of the Detroit River, which drains all the upper Great Lakes. On the eighth day of August 1764, we reached the beleaguered fortress of Detroit without facing opposition.

In fact, Detroit was far from a fortress; it would better be described as a fortified town that consisted of four streets divided by a central avenue into ten blocks of houses and shops. The whole was surrounded by a strong stockade, with a blockhouse in each corner, the latter situated so as to command the exterior walls. The inhabitants were mainly Canadians, so the town people spoke French, and the community itself served the people of the extensive farmsteads along both sides of the Detroit River. It was difficult for us to understand how this weak and isolated British outpost had withstood a fifteen month siege.

As we had hoped, most of Pontiac's forces had by now returned to their distant villages to prepare for the winter, thus abandoning the siege. By early September, General Bradstreet negotiated a peace treaty with the Odawa, Huron, Ojibwe, and Pottawatomi which granted peace while requiring only that the Indians acknowledge themselves to be the subjects of King George and that they surrender all white captives immediately. There was thus no punishment for their attacks on and capture of numerous British military posts or for the death of His Majesty's soldiers or the destruction of Crown property.

While the treaty was being negotiated, I received a startling piece of intelligence concerning my goods and peltries that had been plundered at Fort Michilimackinac. I was approached on the street by a small-time Canadian trader by the name of Amable Deniviere, whom I vaguely recognized from Michilimackinac. He was a very large fellow with a thick black beard that hid a rather handsome face. I thought at once that he had the shifty eyes and confident *braggado* of a swindler. In this opinion, I was later justified. M. Deniviere first asked if I was, indeed, M. Henry, late of Michilimackinac and, being assured that I was, confided that he had valuable information for me. First, however, he required a tankard of rum to loosen his tongue. My curiosity piqued; I invited him to join me for a drink in a nearby tavern on Rue Saint Jacques. After his tongue was well loosened, he spun out his tale which on first telling, I found barely credible as much as I wanted to believe him.

He asked me to recall the night after the attack when traders, surviving soldiers, and the Canadian inhabitants had been closed into the fort without any Indians present. In the terror and confusion of that night, he and his friend M. Cote took the opportunity to break into the trader storerooms and homes and to steal away as many of their trade goods and pelts as they could find. He told me that most of my own goods were plundered in this fashion. He freely admitted that their motive was to enrich themselves before the Indians returned and thoroughly searched the fort for English goods. A snag arose in their plan when their priest, Fr. Du Jaunay, discovered their activities. The priest, realizing the broader implication of the theft, ordered the two of them to surrender the plundered goods to him for safekeeping. Fr. Du Jaunay made them hide the stolen goods in the one place inside the fort where the Indians would not search, namely a large log burial crypt which lay under the altar of Saint Anne's Church. The crypt was not generally known, but even if discovered, it contained the bones of the dead that were much feared by native people.

"Why," I asked Deniviere, "are you confessing your part in this affair to me now?" He said that since the Canadians inside the fort had stood by during the Indian attack and had not helped the soldiers, the new English commandant would not look with favor on Canadians when he was approving new permits to trade with the Indians. "Perhaps," he said, "you would put forward a recommendation in favor of me and M. Cote." I told him that if I recovered my property, I would think about it.

Given the possibility that I might yet be able to recover some of my goods and pelts, I determined to return immediately to Fort Michilimackinac. Soon after my conversation with M. Deniviere, I learned that General Bradstreet was sending Capt. William Howard to garrison Fort Michilimackinac, and I applied to go with him as a guide and interpreter. This request was granted, and I prepared for the journey. In the second week of September, our fleet of eight large longboats and two Canadian bateaux carrying together sixty soldiers of the Seventeenth Regiment of Foot set out across Lake Saint Clair. The shores of the Detroit River and the lake were all cultivated in a pattern of long narrow strip farms of the French tradition. Reaching the outfall of the Saint Clair River into Lake Saint Clair, we found our way impeded by a large sandbar which required us to drag our boats through shallow water. We then proceeded up the clear and beautiful blue Saint Clair River until we reached the south end of Lake Huron. Here, the local Indians, who lived in large villages on both banks, had established a very productive fishery using nets weighted with very large anchor stones to keep them in place in the swift current of the river. We traded for whitefish, pike, and a species of trout.

Our course north followed the west shore of Lake Huron that was cloaked with mounds of greenery from its vast hardwood forests. In due course, we reached a deep and broad embayment called Saginaw Bay. It being a day with scant wind, the captain decided to cross the mouth rather than stick to the coastline. The crossing, according to our crude map, was a distance of twenty-five miles over open water. Midway across, we were glad to put ashore and rest on a rocky island which the voyagers call Charity Isle. Setting out again to the northwest, we struck the mainland and, as before, followed the coast to the north. Now the hardwood forests began showing the darker green of towering pine trees and the stark white of the birch.

The next landmark was a large shallow bay called by the Ojibwe *Animiki* or the "bay of the thunderbirds" because this region is thought to be the abode of these mythological creatures. This area is also believed to be frequented by the thunderbird's mortal enemies, the underwater panther, *Mishipishieu*. The Indians say that the thunder, so frequently heard rolling across the water of this bay, is made by the flapping of the giant bird's wings, and the flashing lightning strikes are thunderbolts thrown by the *Animiki* at the dreaded *Mishipishieu*. Needless to say, Thunder Bay is a dangerous place. The Ojibwe, who are planning to paddle across these waters, try to avert the threat of the underwater *manitou* by leaving offerings at large spirit rocks. These rocks are located at the south and north points of land which bracket the bay. We rested at *Negwegon* on the south point, where we observed strange rock alignments before making the seven mile crossing. On reaching north point, I examined the spirit rock and discovered that it is actually composed of four large rocks surrounded by many smaller stones. The Indians say the large rocks have been here forever but that the smaller stones have come to join them more recently. The ground around the large stones is littered with tobacco, bits of iron, pieces of old kettles, pipes, and various other offerings left by travelers. Michilimackinac is about one hundred miles northwest of the north point of Animiki Bay.

The fact that we had seen no Indians and only deserted villages since leaving the Saint Clair River gave evidence that the passage of our force had been foretold and that our progress had been noted by eyes from the dark forested shores. This conclusion gave the ever vigilant Capt. Howard pause for fear that his troops might be headed for an ambush, or at least a hostile reception when landing at the fort. Rather than be surprised, he decided to disembark his troops at the mouth of the Black River and march his soldiers the last dozen miles to Fort Michilimackinac. This was accomplished without molestation from the Indians, and we arrived at the gates of the fort in the evening.

CHARLES CLELAND

Actually, the Canadians and the few Indians residing around the fort were very welcoming and hopeful that all would be forgiven. Capt. Howard promptly summoned the Odawa from L'Arbre Croche, and they soon appeared bringing several Ojibwe chiefs as well. A peace was concluded with both groups.

My immediate interest, of course, was to investigate M. Deniviere's wild tale with the possibility of recovering my property. I wasted no time in going to the priest's house located just north of the Saint Anne's Church. Fr. Du Jaunay, who occupied the dwelling, was well versed in the complex politics the Great Lakes frontier and also maintained excellent relationships with the British military, his Canadian parishioners, and, to some degree, with the local Indians.

When I appeared at his door, he no doubt guessed my mission, and he quickly verified that he, indeed, held some of my goods and pelts which, as he put it, he "managed to snatch from the Ojibwe just before they ransacked the entire fort looking for plunder." As the priest related his story, he found several of his Canadian parishioners looting the storehouses and homes of the English traders. Although he knew the Indians would be blamed for the theft, he also believed that the true identity of thieves would eventually be revealed when the English regained the fort. If this were the case, punishment would fall on all the Canadians, and they would likely be barred from the fur trade, thus being deprived of their livelihood. With this conclusion in mind, he ordered the culprits to collect all the goods and furs and to bring them to the church. With the help of several trusted parishioners, he hid them beneath the church.

The father then led me into the church and pointed out a cleverly concealed trap door in the floor near the altar. Once opened, a hole was revealed with a ladder that descended into the dark between bark-lined walls. Father supplied me with a candle, and I descended step by step into the stale gloom of a log-lined burial chamber. In the dim and sputtering candlelight, I could make out only a single coffin resting on a scaffold; otherwise, the crypt was completely empty. My heart sank with deep disappointment.

Just then, Fr. Du Jaunay called down to me, "No, not down there, behind the bark." I climbed part way up the ladder and removed a large piece of bark from the lining of the shaft. This revealed a huge space between the ground level and the floor of the sanctuary above, the floor being built on a stone foundation about three feet above the ground. In this space, I could see all manner of bales, boxes, and casks. Crawling among this assortment, I examined the lead baling seals attached to various containers and found among them the six-pointed star which marked the property of Ezekiel Solomon, my own AH cartouche, as well as the seals of other traders. I was overjoyed to have recovered most of my property and grateful to Fr. Du Jaunay for saving it.

My gratitude led me to ask him if I could make a gift to the church of 10 percent of the value of my recovered property. The wily father thought for a moment and replied that 20 percent would be a more generous gift to further God's work. I countered this suggestion with an offer of 15 percent and a promise to put in a good word with Capt. Howard about the behavior the Canadians. The priest extended his hand to seal our bargain.

The season was now progressing, but I still had the opportunity to extend goods on credit to fourteen Indian families leaving for their winter hunting grounds as well as to outfit a group of Canadian traders heading for La Baye on the west side of *Michigami*. I also wrote to my partner M. Campion, as well as to my friend and competitor Ezekiel Solomon, alerting him to his great good fortune. I sent these letters down country with a returning canoe brigade, and I hoped that they would result in a spring shipment of supplies and trade goods, which would permit me to enter the trade.

While searching through my recovered goods, I was overjoyed to find a very expensive item that I had ordered from France before the attack, but for which I now had an urgent need. Inside a beautifully finished walnut box with brass hinges and clasp was an exquisite pair of French dueling pistols with finely engraved side plates; the firearms and powder flask were set amid a plush green velvet lining.

I had one more voyage to make before the stormy weather on the lakes made travel overly risky. Accordingly, I acquired a place in one of the canoes headed for La Baye on the west shore of *Michigami*. I also took with me several bales of dried lake trout, which I hoped to trade at La Baye for a supply of wild rice that abounds in that region. We set out on October 2 under a deep blue sky with a fresh breeze out of the southwest and three-foot waves.

CHAPTER 16

THE THREE CANOES of our brigade paddled across the Straits of Mackinac and turned west skirting the north coast of *Michigami*. This was the route of the voyagers heading either south to the Illinois country by way of the lake or to the valley of the Wisconsin River and the upper Mississippi valley to the west. This course would eventually put us in the lee of the western shore of the lake, where travelers were sheltered from the prevailing west winds that blow constantly across *Michigami*. We were not sheltered, however, for the first part of our portion of the voyage; and as we progressed westward, we encountered waves driving the entire length of the lake. These were closely spaced four-foot swells that caused our canoe to roll from side to side. I was soon seasick, and my vomiting and retching produced smirks on the faces of our tough, seasoned Canadian paddlers.

The place names along the passing shore speak to the Canadian tradition of those who are its most frequent travelers. We passed, in turn, Gros Cap, Pointe aux Chenes, Epoufette, Milicoquins, Seul Choix, and Manistique. Finally, we came to a large peninsula extending south into the lake. Given the high seas, we decided to make a portage across the peninsula and, after landing, followed a well-beaten path from Portage Bay a few miles to Bay de Noc on the other side of the peninsula. As we continued south along the shore, we encountered a forbidding Indian rock painting that the local Indians say has very ancient origins.

The painting is located next to a shallow cave, whose mouth is fifteen feet above the water. The painting itself, rendered in bright red ocher, shows a very fat human form with stubby arms and legs and a pointed head. Lines extend from his umbilicus, arms and legs and curve around his body, terminating in a huge sixteen-legged spider like creature. As we cruised close to this painting, several of the voyagers fired their muskets into the cave. This, they explained, was an ancient tradition that Indians of olden times initiated by shooting arrows in the same manner to assure us safe passage.

Leaving the peninsula, we paddled south, passing one island after another, until we arrived at the largest island that lies between *Michigami* and the mouth of Green Bay. We paddled west, passing through a narrow strait called *Porte de Morts* or death's door and entered Green Bay. The shores of Green Bay are in the country of the Menominee or the wild rice people. The peninsula that separates *Michigami* from Green Bay is, however, also occupied by the Potawatomi people as well as the Menominee.

Our route took us south on the placid waters of Green Bay, until we reached its end where the Fox River flows out from a large fertile valley. Upriver, the Fox flows through several lakes which, in turn, connect with the short portage that gives access to the Wisconsin River, which ultimately flows west into the upper Mississippi River. At the place where the Fox River enters Green Bay, the French had built a small fort on its west shore in order to control access to this important waterway. The fort, called La Baye, was lost to the French following the fall of New France, after which time it was briefly occupied by the British Army. The British abandoned La Baye in 1763 during the Pontiac rebellion and had not since garrisoned it. During the years of French control, Agustin de Langlade and his son Charles founded a trading post here, and that establishment attracted Canadian men who soon began to marry Menominee women.

The *métis* community that resulted is today composed of several large families. The Brunet, Lagral, and Joseph Roy families reside on the western side of the Fox, while the de Langlade, Grignon, Amable Roy, and Merchand families reside on the eastern side. Together, these families, their Canadian *engages* and *panis* servants add up to fifty-six people. Of course, many of the seven families are intermarried and are also united with the Menominee families and their associated clans of the tribe. Although the families of the *métis* community cultivate large gardens and orchards, their main occupation is trading in furs. Many of the men labor as *engagees* to the fur merchants, transporting furs and goods back and forth to Montréal, and they also sometimes overwinter in Indian camps where they bargain for newly trapped furs. Their Indian or *métis* wives tend their homes and children, plant and care for the gardens, raise chickens and pigs, and make many handicraft items necessary to support trading ventures. The *metis* are devoted Catholics and maintain separate identities appropriate to the distinct communities within which they normally interact.

Charles de Langlade or *Akewaugetauso,* as he is known among the Indians, and who is also the object of my visit to La Baye, is a perfect example. His mother was the daughter of the Odawa chief, *Nisowaquet,* whom the Canadians called La Fourche. Incidentally, *Nisowaquet* was one of the very chiefs who rescued me from the Ojibwe after the attack at Michilimackinac. *Nisowaquet* trained his grandson, young Charles, as a warrior from a very early age; and as a young man, Charles led Odawa war parties in battles during many engagements of the French and Indian wars. In 1760, he was appointed as a lieutenant in the French Army and was ordered to command French troops at Fort Michilimackinac. It was Charles who surrendered that post to the British Army in 1763 and, thereafter, served the British interest, including giving Capt. Etherington repeated warnings of the impending Indian attack, which he ignored. Soon after the attack, de Langlade moved his family from Michilimackinac to La Baye where he was appointed by the British as the Superintendent of the Indians of the Green Bay Department. Although he sometimes resided at Fort Michilimackinac, where he owned a house, his main residence was at La Baye where he continued to engage in the fur trade. By any measure, Charles de Langlade is a towering figure on the Great Lakes frontier.

We, of course, knew each other from my time trading at Michilimackinac and our encounter during the Indian attack. As much as I respected de Langlade's accomplishments, I was haunted by the single sentence he uttered when I had begged him to preserve my life during the heat of the slaughter and my despair. At this, he shrugged his shoulders, turned his back to me, and said, *"Que voudriez-vous que j'enferais?"* (What do you want me to do about it?)

Even then, I knew that he had the prestige and influence among the Indians to protect me from the fiercest warriors. This single incident cast a cloud over my opinion of the great man.

After several days' residence in the area, when de Langlade had certainly heard of the presence of *Zhigaag,* I knocked on the door of M. de Langlade. It was opened by his wife, Charlotte, who greeted me as if I were expected, and offered me a mug of fresh cider, which I readily accepted. Their home was neat, clean, and well furnished. Charles soon appeared and greeted me graciously. He knew of my good fortune in recovering my goods and praised the action of Fr. Du Jaunay. Both he and Madame de Langlade were anxious for news of their friends at Michilimackinac and especially of my opinion of Capt. Howard.

At length, I mentioned the reason for my visit. I said that I wished to purchase the *pani* woman, Josette, who hid me during the attack. I knew that Madame de Langlade had two *panis* slaves, but she was quick to oppose the selling of Josette, saying she could not possibly get along with only one servant. But ever the businessman, de Langlade asked what I would give for her.

At this point, I reached into my tote bag and brought out the box containing the dueling pistols. I immediately had his attention, and before opening the box, I increased his curiosity as well as his anticipation by telling him about my great difficulty and expense of obtaining this treasure. I slowly opened the box, and as his eyes moved over the twin firearms with their elaborately engraved silver side and butt plates, I could see that he was enthralled, as could Madame, and she began to protest anew. De Langlade silenced her with a dark look and picked up one of the pistols, weighing its perfect balance in his hand. After a thorough inspection, including the touch marks of a well-known Parisian gunsmith stamped into the barrels of each gun, he said I must come back tomorrow, while he considered the offer; I packed up the pistols and departed.

On the following day, I was back at the de Langlade's door and was again seated at the table by a very sour looking Madame de Langlade. When M. de Langlade appeared and settled in a chair, he said that I had disturbed his domestic tranquility and that he wanted to acquire the pistols, but perhaps I might offer something more to soothe his household. I was prepared with a counter offer. I explained to him that on my return to Fort Michilimackinac, I was going to apply for a trader's license, which Capt. Howard had offered me as a payment for my services as a guide and interpreter when we traveled from Detroit. I told him I was considering asking for one of two locations, either the Lake Superior country or La Baye. Now it was M. de Langlade who had the sour face. My offer was that he would take the pistols and that I would take Josette and go to Lake Superior. He quickly agreed, as I knew he would, since the last thing he wanted was the competition of a well-financed English trader in his midst. Monsieur then announced

CHARLES CLELAND

that one other matter remained, and at that, he summoned Josette who entered the room and smiled in my direction. De Langlade then asked her if she would be willing to be sold to M. Henry. Josette appeared to be flustered by being asked to make such a decision, but much to my joy and satisfaction, she agreed. By leaving the decision to Josette who was, after all, a slave in their household, my regard for the de Langlades rose to new heights. Clearly they had much affection for Josette.

Josette soon appeared with a small bundle containing her possessions, and I handed over the pistol box to de Langlade; Madame was weeping, and I was further impressed by her attachment to Josette. The two women clung to each other for a moment, and then the two of us went out the door.

Josette and I crossed to the west side of the Fox River, where I had taken temporary lodging in the household of Pierre Grignon. Here, Josette and I had a serious discussion about the future. Since her Ojibwe was better than my poor French, we decided to communicate in Ojibwe, although she asked me to begin teaching her English. Since I had long had Josette on my mind, I told her right off that she was no longer a slave but a free woman. I said I hoped she would be my partner in life, and although I would not marry her in the Catholic Church, I hoped we would have a marriage "*a la facon du pays*," that is, a customary marriage, such as is common on the frontier. Josette told me that what occurred today was her dream come true and that after our brief tryst at Fort Michilimackinac, she had often thought about me and even dared to hope that I might someday come for her. She said that she was not concerned with marriage or the concerns of the Catholic fathers, but she was overjoyed to be a free person and that she was happy to live as my companion and partner.

The next day, as we prepared to go back to Michilimackinac, my first task was to trade my smoked fish for wild rice. M. Grignon recommended a certain Menominee, who could supply me with the one hundred pounds of rice I sought. Josette and I finally found him and were soon engaged in bargaining. He offered fifty pounds of rice for my fish, and I was ready to accept the offer. Just then, Josette forcefully entered the discussion and speaking in the Menominee dialect, called the man a thief, telling him my good Mackinac trout were worth one hundred and fifty pounds of rice, but that we would take only one hundred pounds as a favor to him, as he was a relative of our friend,

Pierre Grignon. At this, he agreed to our one-hundred-pound offer, and we exchanged commodities. I had a flush of satisfaction at how vigorously my new partner represented our interest and how good was the bargain I had made with M. de Langlade. Later that same day, we found two Canadian voyagers who wanted to return to Mackinac Island to winter with their *métis* families, and I purchased a twenty-foot canoe in decent shape for the return trip. The October weather, being unusually warm and calm, we decided to leave early the next morning; and at sunrise, we set out to retrace my trip of ten days earlier. With a light load and four paddlers, we made excellent time and reached Michilimackinac in six days. I sold the canoe to our two Canadian companions who continued on to their waiting families.

While there, I was greatly surprised to meet my brother *Miigwan* near the fort and to learn that *Wawatum* was camped nearby with the entire family. I had expected that they would have gone south to their winter hunting grounds. As it turned out, they had decided to stay at the Straits of Mackinac this fall in order to fish for whitefish and lake trout and then to winter in the Saint Mary's River valley. *Miigwan* took us to their wigwam, and they were all as surprised and happy to see me as I was to see them. I introduced Josette, and in a short while, *Wabigonkwe* and *Anangons* duly incorporated her into their activities, and soon they were soon chatting and joking like old friends. *Wawatum* then invited us to stay with them, to which I readily agreed. Baby *Papakins*, my little niece, was now a walker and was very busily running back and forth on unsteady legs pointing at every object with her little nose and asking *wa wa*? or "what is this?" She truly reminded me of a little grasshopper, for which she was named. Naturally, she did not recognize me but soon warmed to my presence and reached out her little arms begging to be picked up.

From our first evening in the *Wawatum* lodge, the family enjoyed telling Josette of my misadventures. *Miigwan* reported the look of horror on my face when I thought I might have to immediately marry *Anangons*'s sister. My mother, *Wabigonkwe*, described my first dog feast and how I had to be coaxed to even taste the fat little puppy she had roasted in my honor. *Wawatum* detailed how I'd gotten lost in the woods and finally found my way back yapping like a coyote and hungry as a starving bear. Josette much enjoyed these glimpses into my checkered past, and even I could not help but join in their raucous laughter.

The next morning, I was sought out by Capt. Howard's adjutant and was surprised to be handed two letters, which had arrived for me with military dispatches from Detroit. The first was from my cousin Collin, informing me that he was accepting my invitation to teach him the fur trade; and after his enlistment ended, he would arrive on the first boat bound for Michilimackinac in the spring.

The second letter was posted in Montréal by my partner M. Etienne Champion. He congratulated me on my escape from the troubles at the fort, of which he had a full account from my friend Ezekiel Solomon, who was now in temporary residence in that city. He said he was horrified by our experience and narrow escape. He also reported that he had met with our bankers and arranged credit. In the early spring, he would send four canoe loads of merchandise, valued at ten thousand pounds of beaver. I was stunned by this good news, since with this shipment, plus the goods I recovered, I would likely be the largest independent trader in the Great Lakes country.

In order to fulfill my promise to Fr. Du Jaunay, I sought and was granted an interview with Capt. Howard. I was ushered into his office, and he greeted me warmly. I soon fulfilled my promise to Fr. Du Jaunay by complimenting the behavior of the Canadians in saving my goods and those of the other English traders. (I did not tell him that they had stolen these goods before saving them.) I also explained that, while the Canadians had not taken up arms in our behalf because they had not been attacked, they had hidden both Solomon and me in their homes, thus saving us from certain death. In addition, I made the case that the Canadians were indispensable to the operation of the fur trade, and they should not be punished by limiting their participation. Capt. Howard seemed to agree with my assessment, but no doubt, Fr. Du Jaunay had already made this same case with him.

I then reminded the commandant of his promise to grant me a trading license for the 1765 season. For some time I had contemplated trying a new territory, and my good *ami* Jean-Baptiste Cadotte had filled my head with stories about the immense beaver populations in the Lake Superior country. I decided to ask to be given a monopoly to trade on Lake Superior. He readily agreed, and I was gratified by the chance to rebuild my business in a new and exciting region with unlimited possibilities.

That evening, I discussed my plans and prospects with Josette and my Ojibwe family. We were all excited. We agreed that Josette and I would winter in Sault Sainte Marie and spend the time finding or building a store, a storage building, and an office for our new enterprise. When Collin arrived, we would send him into the woods with *Miigwan* to learn the fundamental skills of survival and trapping; and upon his return to the Sault, he would become the clerk in our store and keep our books. In the meantime, Josette and I would spend the summer exploring the Lake Superior shoreline and visiting the Ojibwe summer villages to locate the best places to send our Canadian *engagees* to collect fur the following winter. *Wawatum* and the family would reside near the Sault to fish, make sugar, build canoes, and make other handicrafts to support our brigades. Finally, we would all share in the profits of our enterprise. *Wawatum* and I were both looking forward to spending time together, and I was especially glad to have Josette at my side.

HISTORICAL NOTES

H ISTORICAL FICTION, BY its very nature, requires a blending of historic fact with fictional embellishment. In the case of Alexander Henry's travels and adventures, I endeavored to remain true to the times and places he described in his memoir, as well as the historical characters with whom he interacted.

Alexander did leave New Jersey in 1760 to follow Gen. Amherst's army up the Mohawk trail to Oswego, and he was with the army when it attacked Fort Levi. Later, after losing his goods in the Saint Lawrence River, he made his way to Montréal and acquired Etienne Campion as his fur trade partner. Resupplied with trade goods, he ascended the Ottawa River with his canoe brigade to the Upper Lakes country. Arriving at Fort Michilimackinac as the first British trader to appear in what had been the domain of the French, he was greeted with hostility by the local Ojibwe who were strong allies of the French. After escaping a fire in Sault Sainte Marie, the Indian attack and capture of Fort Michilimackinac and a night in a burial cave on Mackinac Island, he continued his travels as an adopted member of the *Wawatum* family. While on the family's winter hunting ground in central Lower Michigan, he was lost for a time in the winter woods and did shoot a huge bear, while otherwise participating in the everyday aspects of Ojibwe life. On the family's return to Michilimackinac that spring, he participated in a panther hunt, the death and burial of a child, and the mysterious predictions of an Ojibwe seer.

Over this basic framework, I have provided dialogue and fuller descriptions of the places Henry visited as well as the activities that were part of his travels. Since nothing is known of Henry's life prior to his twenty-first birthday, one wonders how he became interested in travel and in deciding to become a fur trade merchant. These are problems for the writer to solve. While he did travel to the Mohawk trail, he was not set upon by deserters, nor did he receive a wound, and therefore no "skunk hair" sprouted from his scalp. Consequently, he was not known to the Indians as *Zhigaag*, although he most assuredly had an Ojibwe nickname.

After his capture by the Ojibwe warriors following the attack on Fort Michilimackinac, *Wenniway* and Henry had a hostile relationship, but Alex did not kill him. As far as we know, the *Wawatum* family never visited Ottawa Island (known today as Drummond Island), nor did Henry get sick on his visit to that place. Had he been sick, treatment would have been as here described.

A pani slave girl did hide Alex and probably saved his life during the Indian attack on Fort Michilimackinac. As far as we know, he did not have a personal relationship with her, nor did he buy her from Charles de Langlade.

In 1764, Henry was refinanced and again entered the fur trade, but he never recovered any of his goods which were plundered during the attack. His new venture was centered in the Lake Superior basin and in Central Canada.

I hope that the fictional aspects of my account will add to the reader's interest and to Henry's own description, including the nature of Ojibwe and Odawa culture as it was in the mid-eighteenth century. I have not embellished the intrepid character who was the real Alexander Henry.

It is not known how Henry met *Wawatum*, his friend and benefactor. Henry did not save *Wawatum* and his wife from a panther attack.

BIBLIOGRAPHY

Adams, James T. D., ed.
1944 *Album of American History. Volume 1, Colonial Period.* New York: Charles Scribner's Sons

Armour, David, ed.
1971 *Attack at Michilimackinac.* Mackinac Island State Park Commission, Mackinac Island: Trikraft Incorporated

Armour, David and K. R. Widder
1978 *At the Crossroads: Michilimackinac During the American Revolution.* Mackinac Island: Mackinac Island State Park Commission

Baraga, Fredrick
1973 *A Dictionary of the Otchipwe Language.* Minneapolis: Ross & Haines Incorporated

Borneman, Walter R.
2006 *The French and Indian War.* New York: Harper and Collins

Brown, Jennifer S. H. and Robert Brightman
1988 *"The Orders of the Dreamed": George Nelson on Cree and Northern Ojibwa Religion and Myth, 1823.* Saint Paul: The Minnesota Historical Society Press

Carufel, D., R. Chapman, J. Chosa, C. Defoe
1992 *Waswaaganing Ojibwemowin, Ojibwe Language Manual.* Lac du Flambeau, Wisconsin: Family Circles AODA Prevention Program.

Dary, David
2009 *Frontier Medicine.* New York: Alfred A. Knoph

Densmore, Francis
1970 *Chippewa Customs.* Minneapolis: Ross & Haines Incorporated

Dunnigan, Brian
2008 *A Picturesque Situation, Mackinac before Photography 1615–1860.* Detroit: Wayne State University Press

Eccles, W. J.
1998 *The French in North America 1500–1783.* East Lansing: Michigan State University Press

Eklund, Coy
1991 *Chippewa (Ojibwe) Language Book.* New York: privately printed

Grignon, Augustine
1904 Seventy-two years recollections of Wisconsin. *Collections of the State Historical Society of Wisconsin*, volume 3, pp. 197–295. Madison

Grim, John A.
1983 *The Shaman, Patterns of Siberian, and Ojibway Healing.* Norman: University of Oklahoma Press

Henry, Alexander
1809 *Travels and Adventures in Canada and the Indian Territories 1760–1776.* New York: I. Riley

Howard, James H.
1965 *The Ponca Tribe.* Smithsonian Institution, Bureau of American Ethnology, Bulletin 195. Washington DC: US Government Printing Office

Huck, Barbara
2000 *Exploring the Fur Trade Routes of North American.* Winnipeg: Heartland

Ilko, John A.
1995 *Ojibwa Chiefs 1690–1890.* Troy New York: The Whitston Publishing Company

Innis, Harold A.
1930 *The Fur Trade in Canada*. Toronto: University of Toronto Press.

Jameson, Ann
1838 *Winter Studies and Summer Rambles in Canada*. Volume 3,
London: Saunders and Otley

Johnston, Basil
1976 *Ojibway Heritage*, Toronto: McClelland and Stewart Incorporated

Johnston Basil
1995 *The Manitous*. New York: Harper Collins Publishers

Katz Irving I.
1948 Ezekiel Solomon: The First Jew in Michigan. *Michigan History Magazine*.

Landis, Ruth
1997 *The Ojibway Woman*. Lincoln: University of Nebraska Press

Litin, Scott C., ed.
2003 *Mayo Clinic Family Health Book*. New York: Harper Collins Publishers

Luzader, John F.
2001 *Fort Stanwix: Construction and Military History*. Rome New York: Fort Stanwix National Monument

Meeker, James, Joan Elias, J. A. Heim
1993 *Plants Used by the Great Lakes Ojibwa*. Odanah, WI: Great Lakes Indian Fish and Game Commission

Morris, Eric W.
1969 *Fur Trade Canoe Routes of Canada, Then and Now*. Ottawa: National and Historic Parks Branch, Ministry of Indian Affairs and Northern Development

Peckham, Howard
1947 *Pontiac and the Indian Uprising.* Princeton NJ: Princeton University Press

Quimby, George I.
1962 A Year with a Chippewa Family, 1763–1764. *Ethnohistory,* volume 9(3)

Quimby, George I.
1966 *Indian Culture and European Trade Goods.* Madison: University of Wisconsin Press

Reeder, Red
1972 *The French and Indian War.* Quechee, Vermont: Heritage Press.

Smith, Teresa S.
1995 *The Island of the Anishnaabeg.* Moscow: University of Idaho Press

Stone, Lyle M.
1994 *Fort Michilimackinac 1715–1781: An Archaeological Perspective on the Revolutionary Frontier.* East Lansing: Anthropological Series, Volume 2, Publications of the Museum, Michigan State University

Widder, Keith
2013 *Beyond Pontiac's Shadow.* East Lansing: Michigan State University Press.

CHARLES CLELAND

58293326R00095

Made in the USA
Lexington, KY
08 December 2016